# Cathy Hopkins

# *Mates, Dates & Sizzling Summers*

PICCADILLY PRESS • LONDON

*This book is for my dad, Wilf Hopkins (aka Billy Hopkins) whose short stay in hospital the year before last inspired many of the scenes in this book. Not the part about TJ's dad being a grumpy old wrinkly. Er . . . not those, course not. Thanks, as always, to Brenda Gardner, Melissa Patey and all the fab team at Piccadilly. And thanks to Steve Lovering for his constant support and help with all aspects of the book.*

First published in Great Britain in 2006
by Piccadilly Press Ltd.,
5 Castle Road, London NW1 8PR
www.piccadillypress.co.uk
This edition published 2007

ISBN: 978 185340 938 7 (trade paperback)

3 5 7 9 10 8 6 4

Printed in the ...

# Chapter 1

# Post-Party

'I tell you, that boy was smitten,' said Izzie as she kicked her shoes off and flopped down on my bed. 'S.M.I.T. Smitten.'

I stood in front of the mirror that hung on the back of my bedroom door and frowned at my reflection. 'Nah. He couldn't be. I mean, look at me. Pale face, spot threatening to erupt on my forehead, bags under my eyes . . . No, this is not a look that smits, smites, or whatever the word is. And a boy like Ollie Axford would never fancy me. Not if he knew me properly. No, it was that top you made me wear, Lucy – I felt like I was walking about in my underwear! Every boy in the place was staring at me . . . or rather at my chest.'

Nesta laughed as she reached into her jeans' pocket to pull out some lip-gloss. 'Not to mention all the dads,' she said as she sprawled next to Izzie and began to apply the strawberry-scented lip-gloss.

'It was soooo embarrassing,' I said. 'Never again.'

Lucy took a pillow off the bed and made herself comfortable on the floor next to my dog, Mojo. 'You looked fab,' she said as she tickled Mojo's ears. 'It showed off your shape, that's all. You should wear things like that more often instead of those tracksuits that you hide away in.'

'I don't hide away in them. They're comfortable.'

Nesta pulled a face and put her gloss away. 'And dead boring. You always amaze me, TJ. You've got gorgeous brown eyes, a mouth most actresses would kill for and great legs. You can look five-star if you want – like you did last night with your hair loose down your back and a bit of make-up on – but most of the time, your hair's scraped back and you slob around in tracksuits like that shapeless grey *thing* you're wearing today.'

'They're cosy and easy to wear,' I retaliated.

'They're passionkillers,' she said. 'If you got it, flaunt it, I say. And you got it, girl.'

You're the ones who've got it, girls, I thought as I looked at the three of them lounging around my room and looking like an ad in a teen mag. Nesta's tall and skinny with long black hair, coffee-coloured skin and fab, high cheek bones; even today when she's only wearing jeans and a T-shirt she still looks stunning. Lucy and Izzie are attractive too but in different ways. Lucy is the smallest of the four of us with short blond hair and Izzie is tall with chestnut-coloured hair, cut in layers down to her shoulders and she's got a gorgeous curvy figure. Boys always look at them wherever we go and I think they're the best-looking bunch at our school. I'm still amazed that they adopted me into their group last year after my best mate, Hannah, went off to live in South Africa.

Izzie pushed her tummy out over her jeans. 'Yeah. If I had a body like yours, TJ, I think I *would* walk around in my underwear all day with a sign in front saying, *Look at me, I look so fab, look at my flat stomach, look at my legs* . . . la la lahhh . . .'

'You're mad, Izzie Foster,' I said. 'But thank God Mum and Dad weren't there last night. Dad would have had a heart attack!'

It was Sunday, the day after the charity ball that we'd been planning for weeks — all through April — and the girls were round at my house for the post-party gossip.

'It feels strange that it's over after all the work that we've put in,' said Izzie, sighing. 'Bit of an anticlimax. All those weeks of putting up posters, selling tickets, organising the music, the fashion show, trying not to panic when it looked like no one was going to show up . . .'

'Worth it in the end though, hey?' I asked. 'I still can hardly believe that we not only met our fundraising target but surpassed it.'

It had been a great night. Nesta had managed to talk a top model called Star Axford into taking part in the fashion show. Her dad is Zac Axford (the famous rock and roller) and, to everyone's amazement, *he'd* turned up to the show, along with his son Ollie. I noticed Ollie the moment he walked in (tall, dark and buff) and he noticed me (or rather my boobs). We both did a double take and then laughed. After the fashion show he'd asked me to dance, and when he left he'd taken my number.

Lucy is our fashion expert and, as I hadn't found a special outfit, she had dressed me for the occasion. I'd been complaining that I had no waist to speak of so she had risen to the challenge and made me a special corset top designed to give an hourglass figure. It was low at the front and laced up tight at the back and yes, it did give me a waist, but it also gave me the most enormous cleavage. My eyes almost popped out of my head (and my boobs out of the top!) when I saw myself in the mirror at the hall where we got changed.

'The effect of cleavage on boys is funny,' said Nesta. 'Like if you show the tiniest bit, they can't help but stare. It's like an eyeball magnet.'

'The tiniest bit is all you get in my case,' said Lucy. 'And actually, you're right. Boys even stare at *my* chest these days.'

'But seriously,' I said, 'I reckon that's the last we've seen of Ollie Axford.'

'I wouldn't be so sure,' said Nesta. 'I saw the way he looked at you. I bet he calls and asks you out.'

'Nah. He was just passing through,' I said. 'And anyway, he looks like a player. You know the type. Too much of a naughty twinkle in his eye to be trusted. And I bet he likes fun girls. He'd soon get bored with me when he realised how straight and sensible I am.'

'You're not straight and sensible,' said Nesta, 'least not all the time.'

'I am,' I said. 'I'm boring.'

'I used to think that you were,' Nesta started, then Lucy thumped her. '*Ow!* Well, I did! Before we hung out, I used to think you were *really* boring, but you're just one of these people who's quiet in the beginning and it takes a while to get to know. Then when you do, you realise they are not boring in the slightest.'

'Steve liked you when he got to know you,' said Lucy. 'Still does I reckon.'

'No. He hardly speaks to me when I see him,' I said.

'Doesn't mean he doesn't still like you,' said Lucy. 'He keeps his feelings hidden.'

I sighed and joined Nesta and Izzie on the bed. 'Boys are so difficult,' I said. 'My whole love life so far has been a disaster.'

It had, too. My first date was with a boy called Scott who was full of himself and tasted of onions when he kissed me. So much for my first snog. *Blargh*. One to remember? I don't think so.

My second boyfriend was Steve. Great friend more than a great passion. We went out for a short while when I was in Year Nine and I felt safe with him. I could be myself and talk to him easily about anything. (With some boys, I go stupid and start talking alien-speak – that's if I get any words out at all.) I hope that we can be friends again one day as I miss our long chats.

After him was Luke . . . not exactly a boyfriend as he was actually seeing Nesta at the time I met him. I fell for him big time – thought he was my soulmate and that he felt the same. He told me that it was over between him and Nesta so I finished with Steve, and then I found out that Luke was lying and I got majorly confused about how I felt about him. When I was with him, I felt like all the clichés in love songs came true and the world was a happier place. Not that I was happier, though. No. He totally did my head in, but I haven't felt what I felt with him since. Just a glance from him and I used to feel like I was a marshmallow melting. As a kisser, he rated eleven out of ten. Even thinking about kissing him still makes my toes curl up. There was something really special there, but . . . it was a mess. Such a mess. I couldn't trust him and I almost lost Nesta as a friend. I still feel sad that things didn't work out differently.

So, disastrous love life? Yes, I'd say so.

And now Ollie Axford. Very cute and he looks bright, like he's got a brain. But would he be another heartbreaker? I don't think I could bear to go through what I went through with Luke again.

'Not all boys are difficult,' said Nesta, picking up on my thoughts. 'They're not all like Luke.'

Lucy squeezed Nesta's foot. 'Nesta's in lu-hurve.'

Nesta smiled. 'It's true. I am. William Lewis, I loooooove yooooooou. It's amazing.'

'William,' said Izzie, thoughtfully. 'Do you realise that if you married him, and he took your surname, then he'd be William Williams?'

'Yes, but I'm not going to marry him. And even if I did, why would he take my surname?'

Lucy rolled her eyes. 'I can't believe that you're talking about marriage when you've only just started going out with him. And you're only fifteen.'

'Sixteen in August,' said Nesta. 'But I agree. I want to have had lots of boyfriends before I finally settle down, and that's if I ever do. I might just go from one boy to another, gathering experience, and then I'll write my memoirs.'

'Memoirs of a slu-urt,' said Lucy, teasing.

Nesta threw a pillow at her. 'You're the slut – stringing my poor brother along the way you do . . .'

We all laughed. Lucy had an ongoing off-on relationship with Tony, Nesta's brother, but we all knew that it wasn't a case of Lucy stringing him along. She really liked him. And he really liked her. He'll be off to university in September though, so depending on which one he gets into, they might not see much of each other because of the distance – which explains why Lucy doesn't want to get too involved. Bit too late for that though, if you ask me. You only have to see them together to see how besotted they both are.

'What about you, Izzie?' said Lucy. 'See anyone you fancied last night?'

'Zac Axford,' said Izzie wistfully. 'I love that jaded-rock-star look.'

'That's because he is a jaded rock star,' said Nesta. 'He must be in his forties at least.'

'And married,' I pointed out.

'A girl can dream, can't she?' said Izzie. 'But apart from him, nope. With my luck with boys lately, anyone would think that I'm destined to be an old maid.'

Lucy leaned back, took Izzie's hand and looked at her palm. 'I see many boys. Many lovers. In fact, you are ze slut around here and although you try to keep quiet about the fact, we all know it and recommend that you behave yourself. In fact, you should be locked up until you are thirty-five.'

Izzie pulled her hand away. 'Pff. Leave the fortune-telling to me, O mystically challenged one.'

Usually it's Izzie who does all the fortune-telling stuff. She has Tarot cards, crystals and often does our horoscopes for the coming months. Sometimes she even tries out simple spells.

'Let's forget boys for a while,' I said. 'We're here for a purpose. At last, at *laaaaaaast*, Mum has said that I can join the new century and redecorate my room. Don't think Dad's too keen, but then he is stuck in the dark ages.'

'Is he here?' asked Nesta.

I shook my head. 'No, thank God,' I said. 'So we can make as much noise as we like without old misery appearing.'

The girls have been wary of my father ever since he told us off for having a pillow fight the first time they came over. They call him Scary Dad as he can be really intimidating when he wants to be.

'Don't be mean,' said Lucy. 'He's your dad. He can't be that bad.'

'You don't have to live with him,' I said. 'So. Room. What do you think?'

Nesta leaped up from the bed, stepped over Mojo who had fallen asleep on the floor and fetched a carrier bag of things that she'd brought with her.

'Here. Mum gave us loads of mags to look at,' she said as she spread copies of interior design magazines on the bed.

'And I brought my feng shui book,' said Izzie. 'So that the room has the right feel in the end, as well as looking good.'

'Any ideas so far, TJ?' asked Lucy.

'Anything will be an improvement on this,' I said, as I looked around. My room is dull with a capital D. Ancient leafy wallpaper on the walls and a faded cream candlewick bedspread on the bed. When I first became mates with Lucy, Nesta and Izzie and saw their fab bedrooms, I was embarrassed to let them see how old-fashioned our house is. And not just the house, but my parents too. They're a lot older than most people's. In fact, when Nesta first saw them, they were out in the garden and she thought that they were my grandparents. Dad is almost in his seventies and Mum's just turned sixty. I call them the wrinklies. I think it was a shock when Mum realised that she was having me. I think they thought they'd had their family with Marie (who's twenty-seven) and Paul (who's twenty-three), and they had a merry old middle-age to look forward to. Then, surprise! Along I came. What they were doing having sex at their age heaven knows. I don't like to think about it, but they clearly did. And they should have known better than to have an unexpected baby, seeing as both of them are doctors. Dad's a hospital consultant and Mum is a GP. It just goes to show that getting pregnant unexpectedly can happen to anyone, and at any age.

Anyway, neither of them have ever been bothered by décor or having the latest sofa or TV. As long as it all works, Mum always says. Both of them have only just come to terms with e-mail and neither will have a mobile phone. Mum likes to garden in her spare time and Dad likes to read or play golf. So they're not Mr and Mrs Groovacious. Unlike Nesta's parents, for instance. They're both so good-looking and cool. Her dad makes films and TV dramas. Her mum is a newsreader on cable. Lucy's dad runs the health shop in Muswell Hill, but he also plays jazz and teaches the guitar. And her mum is great. She's a counsellor and looks like a children's TV presenter – wearing bright colours that don't quite match. Izzie's parents are straighter. Her mum is an accountant in the City and so is her stepdad. Her real dad is more of a wild card, though – he lectures in English at the university in town and is a great laugh. I like him a lot. We have long conversations about books and he often sends me something to read via Izzie.

'I want colour,' I said and got up to find a book from my desk in the corner. 'This place is soooo bland. I got this book on the Far East out of the library. I love the colours they use over there. Reds, oranges, ochres . . . This side of the house doesn't get much sun so I thought those colours would work better than blues or greens.'

'You could do the room black and white to match Mojo,' said Nesta as Mojo snored in his sleep. 'It's very in to decorate a room to match your pet.'

'Says who?' asked Lucy. 'Some mad journalist who's having a laugh? No. You're right, TJ. Warm colours would be best in here. Make it look cosy. And we could go to Camden Lock and get you an Indian bedspread. Loads of stalls there are selling Eastern stuff at the moment.'

'Yeah,' said Izzie. 'And lanterns. Maybe a little statue of Buddha or the goddess Kali. You could make it look really exotic in here.'

'It's a bedroom, not a temple,' said Nesta. 'She wants some nice cushions, some girlie nick-nacks . . .'

'And some gorgeous fabric at the windows,' said Lucy. 'I used sari material in my room. That would work in here, too. If you go down to Brick Lane they have the most sumptuous colours there: reds threaded with gold, purple with silver edgings. It's going to look great in here.'

'Hey, I haven't got that much money,' I said. 'Mum and Dad don't really believe in spending more than is necessary.'

'Don't worry,' said Lucy. 'There are always ways round it. Markets, ends of rolls, shopping at sale times. We'll make it work within your budget.'

'Which way is west?' asked Izzie, as she got up and pulled a book out of her bag and started flicking through the pages.

I pointed out of the left windowpane. 'That, way, I guess – the sun goes down over there, over the lime trees at the bottom of the garden. How does this feng shui thing work?'

'There are different areas representing different aspects of your life in each room of a property,' Izzie explained. 'An area for career, health, creativity, wealth, relationships and so on. You need a compass and a feng shui book to work out where they fall in each room as it depends on whether a room faces north, south, east or west. And the effect of that can make an area either positive or negative.'

It sounded incredibly complicated to me. I didn't understand a word of it, but didn't like to say as Izzie is so enthusiastic about these sorts of things. 'Er . . . OK. And then what?' I asked.

'Well, for instance, if you have a wealth area in a negative zone where you keep all your savings, accounts, etc. you'd probably find that they didn't do too well. But if you moved them to another room where the wealth area was in a positive space, then they'd probably multiply.'

'Hmm, cool,' I said. 'So what about this room? What's where?'

Izzie consulted her book again. 'Which way does it face again?'

'North,' I said. 'That's why it doesn't get as much light as the front rooms.'

'OK. Good,' said Izzie, flicking the pages and looking around the room. 'Your bed's in a positive creativity place so that's good. You probably have some great ideas when you're falling asleep, yeah?'

I nodded.

And then Izzie let out a soft groan. 'Ohmigod,' she said, as she pointed under my desk. 'Is that where you always keep your bin?'

I nodded again.

'Move it immediately,' she said. 'It's in the relationship area of your life.'

'So why would having the bin there be a problem?'

'It's in a negative zone, so it's like you're putting all your rubbish into your relationships or all your relationships turn to rubbish. It's no wonder things went so weird with Luke. I should have come over and done this for you ages ago! And I would never write any letters to boys you like or take calls from over here,' she said, going to my desk. She began to pull on the desk until it had moved a few feet. 'Here. If we move it over here by the window it will be in a positive career area, plus you'll be able to see outside when you work.'

I picked up the bin. 'And where shall I put this?'

Izzie pointed under the desk. 'You can put that in the career area as well,' she said. 'Just keep the relationship area empty if you can, and don't put a mirror there as it will reflect the negativity.' Izzie looked pleased with herself. 'I think you might find that your relationships take a turn for the better now we've done that.'

Yeah right, I thought. I didn't really believe it myself but I knew that Izzie did, and I didn't want to hurt her feelings.

About two seconds later, the phone rang.

A moment later, Mum called up the stairs. 'TJ, it's for you. Pick up your extension.'

I picked up the phone.

'Hi,' said a male voice. 'Is that TJ Watts?'

'Speaking.'

'Ollie Axford here.'

## Handy Hints for Decorating Your Bedroom

*TJ:* Do your research: get books and magazines on interior design to give you ideas and colour schemes. Try out paint sample pots on the wall to see how the colour looks at different times of the day, and in natural and artificial light.

*Nesta:* Budget. Work out how much you have to spend and save some money for one super duper eye-catching piece, like a jewelled mirror or fab velvet cushion.

*Izzie:* Rule number one in feng shui is clear out the clutter, so get rid of old books, clothes and magazines in order to make way for new ones! Don't forget to make sure that your room smells wonderful. Scented candles and sprays can be used for this. Orange blossom is my current fave.

*Lucy:* Think carefully about your colour scheme, remembering that light colours can open up a room and make it look more airy, whereas dark colours can close it in and make it look smaller but cosier. Gorgeous fabrics can be draped at windows or made into cushions for that finishing touch.

## Colour Ideas

*Cool Colours:* blue and green.

*Warm Colours:* red, orange and yellow.

*Minimal:* white, or shades of white.

*Bright:* vivid pink, lime, yellow, orange and turquoise.

*Fairy Tale:* pastel colours, like pink, pale blue, lilac, lavender and turquoise.

*Romantic:* shades of pink and red.

*Exotic:* spice colours, such as shades of red, all shades of yellow, honey gold and orange.

*Stark:* black and white.

# Chapter 2

# The People Who Live in My Head

'So did he ask you out?' asked Lucy.

I laughed. 'You mean you weren't eavesdropping?'

'As if,' said Nesta. 'No. We respect your privacy. Besides, we couldn't hear through the door when we tried. So did he ask you out?'

'He asked if I could meet him on Wednesday night . . .'

Nesta punched the air. 'Result! Excellent. What will you wear?'

'Well, er . . . I told him I couldn't.'

'Couldn't? Why not?' asked Nesta.

'I want to go up to the bookshop in Muswell Hill. Leila Ferrin is talking. She's one of my favourite authors . . .'

'Let me get this straight. You're going to miss a date with a buff boy because you want to go and hear an author talk?' she asked. 'Er, why?'

'Because I love her books and, as you know, I want to be a

writer and . . . oh, a million reasons. I've been looking forward to it for weeks.'

'Good for you,' said Izzie, then turned to Nesta. 'There is more to life than boys, you know, and you should take a leaf out of TJ's book. Don't drop everything because a boy you fancy comes along. Sometimes they like it when a girl is independent and doesn't just fall at their feet.'

Lucy started laughing. 'A leaf out of TJ's book! Good phrase, seeing as she wants to be a writer!'

Nesta looked peeved. 'I *haven't* fallen at William's feet,' she said. 'You know I haven't. I've played it pretty cool with him. But there's a time to be cool and a time to say, "Hello, sailor, mine's a Diet Coke". And anyway, since when have you been the boy expert round here? That's *my* job!'

It was true. Boy expert was Nesta's post, and usually she was spot-on with advice.

'Exactly,' said Izzie and bowed. 'And you have taught us well, O master. Pity thou canst not follow thy own advice.'

Nesta thumped Izzie over the head with a pillow. 'I am sooooo misunderstood,' she said.

'Did he suggest another time?' asked Lucy.

I shook my head. 'No. Well, actually I probably didn't give him the option. I said that I had friends round so couldn't talk for long. Do you think I've I blown it? I have, haven't I? I've just blown it.'

Nesta shook her head. 'No. If he's interested he will be in touch. That's always the rule. It may take a while, but you'll hear from him again. And actually it might work in your favour that you said no.'

'How?'

'Shows you're not desperate,' said Nesta. 'Most boys hate desperate. So without meaning to, you have played hard to get. Miss Über-Cool. He will probably now see you as a challenge to be conquered. Be prepared to hear from him again.'

'Really?' I said. 'Cool.' I felt chuffed. I thought I couldn't play hard to get if I tried, but there I'd gone and done it without even knowing.

'Anyway, we have work of our own to do in the boy department,' said Nesta. 'Got to go and put our bins in the right place. Come on, Izzie, and bring that fong bong shu book with you.'

'Feng shui,' she said.

'Whatever,' said Nesta. 'I can't risk things going wrong with William, and if it means turning to hocus-pocus, just call me Tabuga the Teenage Witch.'

'Feng shui isn't witchcraft,' said Izzie. 'It's about working with the elements to create harmony . . .'

'Sounds like witchcraft to me,' said Nesta, as she gathered up her bag and headed for the door.

After the girls had gone, I got the bus to Homebase and spent my pocket money on little pots of paint samples of all the spice colours that I'd imagined my room in. When I got back, I had a great time painting squares all over the walls. It was amazing because when the paint dried, the colours looked nothing like the shades on the paint chart. They changed colour again as the sun went down and the light faded in my room.

I looked over at the bin in its new position. Funny that Ollie called as soon as we'd moved it. But if my relationship hopes were going to come true as Izzie had promised, then shouldn't it have been Luke who called, not Ollie?

On Wednesday evening, Mum dropped me at the bookshop and told me to call her when the talk had finished to arrange a lift home, as sometimes these events can go on well after the advertised time. A crowd was already inside milling about, chatting and drinking the wine that was left on a table in the centre of the shop. I helped myself to an orange juice, then went to find a seat in the area at the back of the shop where chairs had been set out in front of the bookshelves. Already most of the good places had been taken, and jackets put on chairs for friends that were late. I should have come earlier, I thought. I should have known a writer as popular as Leila would draw a crowd.

'Hey,' said a voice behind me. 'I was looking for you.'

I turned round and found myself looking into a pair of cornflower-blue eyes. Cute face, too, with a wide smile and a dimple on his chin

It was Ollie Axford. He grabbed my elbow and ushered me to the second row.

'I got here early and nabbed us a good spot,' he said as he pointed to two chairs, one with a jacket on it and the other with a copy of Leila's latest book. We squeezed past people who were already sitting and took our seats.

'But . . . nihwee . . . uh . . . how . . . what are you doing here?' I asked, as inwardly I told myself to calm down. The last thing I wanted was to turn into Noola, my alien alter ego in front of him.

'Come to listen to Leila Ferrin, like you.'

'But . . . how did you know where she was on?'

'You said she was giving a talk on Wednesday night. I bought her book. Called her publisher. They told me where she was talking. Easy.'

'But you didn't mention that you liked her when we spoke on Sunday.'

Ollie grinned and flicked a lock of dark hair out of his eyes. 'No. But I do like one of her readers.'

I felt myself blush – he didn't take his eyes off me when he said this. A moment later, the man who ran the bookshop called for attention and, when the room fell silent, he introduced Leila Ferrin.

I'd seen photos of her on her book covers, but she looked different in the flesh. Older and with salt and pepper hair, but prettier. She was probably in her late fifties or early sixties, with grey-blue eyes. She put on a pair of glasses and scanned the room, taking everyone in.

Once everyone was settled, she spoke for about fifteen minutes about how she got started as a writer, and then did a reading from her latest book, *The People Who Live In My Head*. It was so brilliant I'd read it in three nights. It was about a woman who went on a self-awareness-type course and did an exercise where she had to write down her sub-personalities and give them all names – all the different people she was in different situations. I thought it was a great idea because it's true – our behaviour does change depending on where we are and who we're with and we almost become like different people. In Leila's book, one of the sub-personalities tries to take over and suppress the others and, in the end, all her alter egos gang up on her and then they go into therapy together. Some parts of it were very funny and made me laugh out loud, and other parts made me think. I knew all about sub-personalities because of Noola, the inner alien girl that lives in my head and makes an appearance whenever a cute boy is around. It can be so embarrassing as I start to talk gibberish or alienese.

After the reading, Leila asked the audience if anyone had any questions. I had loads, but felt shy to put my hand up as even just thinking about asking a question made my heart beat faster. Plus Ollie was sitting next to me. I didn't want to make a fool of myself by saying the wrong thing or going blank.

Ollie, on the other hand, wasn't at all shy. His hand shot straight up. 'Were the sub-personalities in your book made up or were they actually yours?'

Leila smiled and raised an eyebrow. 'Well, I'd be giving away a lot if I admitted that they were all mine, wouldn't I? And people might think I was crazy and a half.'

'I wouldn't,' said Ollie. 'I think we all have lots of different sides to us.'

Leila smiled again. 'OK, then let's just say that the characters in the book aren't that far removed from the ones that actually do live in my head.'

Ollie had broken the ice with his question and, after that, loads of people put their hands up asking different things: where she got her inspiration from, how long it took her to write a book, what was she working on next and so on. In the end, she didn't have time to answer all the questions people had, and urged those who hadn't had a chance to speak to her to get in touch through her website.

Excellent, I thought, as I jotted down the website address in the notebook I'd brought. I'd have no problem e-mailing her my question, asking for her top tip for wannabe writers.

After the talk, Ollie and I walked out to the pavement to discover that it had started raining whilst we were inside listening to Leila. Ollie looked over at the café next to the bookshop. 'Got time for a coffee?' he asked. 'My treat.'

I nodded. I could hardly say no after the effort he'd made to see me. I felt flattered that he'd gone to the trouble of not only tracking down where I was going to be, but also doing some homework and buying Leila's book. No boy had ever spent that much time on my behalf before.

'So . . . did you actually read the book?' I asked after we had found a table in the café and put in our orders.

Ollie smiled. 'I do like reading. I read a lot, but it's always good to get a recommendation for a new writer – well, new to me if you know what I mean. You sounded such a fan of Leila's when you spoke about her on the phone. And yes, I did read and enjoy her book.'

The next half an hour flew by as we talked about books, our families, school, our mates and our goals. His life was so different to mine. He was a boarder at a private school in Kensington and his parents live in what sounds like an amazing place down in Cornwall, in a mansion with acres of land. They even have a housekeeper.

'It sounds soooo glamorous,' I said. 'Your dad a rock star and your sister a model and your mum an ex-model. Mine are so boring. Both of them are doctors and their idea of a fun time is listening to Radio Four on a Sunday and pottering in the garden.'

Ollie smiled. 'That's not too far removed from what my mum

and dad like to do. We live a pretty quiet life down there apart from the odd party. Mum loves to throw parties. You should come down sometime, we have loads of spare rooms. You met Star at the do last week, but you could meet my other sister, Lia. She's only a year younger than you.'

Your family are *so* different from mine, I thought. I couldn't imagine ever inviting Ollie to stay with us. For one thing the spare rooms are full of junk and, for another, my Scary Dad doesn't even like my girl friends being over, never mind a boy.

I told Ollie that I wanted to be a writer when I left school and he told me that he was still undecided but might study drama and go into acting. He was so easy to be with, charming and interested in me. Not at all how I'd imagined him when I first met him. I'd thought he might be full of himself, the way some really good-looking boys are.

'So . . .' said Ollie as he paid the bill when we'd finished our drinks. 'You want to be a writer. Have you written down your SPs?'

'SPs?'

'Sub-personalities.'

I laughed. 'Might have done.'

'I did,' he said. 'In the cab on the way up here.' He pulled a piece of paper out of his jacket pocket. 'Want to look?'

'How many are there?'

'Eight,' he said, and began to read his list. '"Son", because I'm one person with my parents. "Friend", because I'm definitely different with my mates to how I am with Mum and Dad. "Casanova" . . ."'

'Casanova?'

'Yeah, my sister Lia calls me that. Casanova with the girls. She's only teasing . . .'

'So why does she call you that? Are you a Casanova?'

'Me. Nah. OK, maybe a little. I like girls' company, that's all. I like talking with them. Boys can be pretty stupid sometimes, and you can have a good conversation with most girls. No crime in that, eh?'

No, I thought. No crime, but I hoped that he wanted more than just a conversation with me.

'OK, so that's three,' I said.

'And then there's "Sports Jock", in fact that personality would be called Jock, then there's my studious side . . .'

'Has he got a name yet?'

'No.'

'Call him Nigel.'

'OK,' said Ollie. 'Nigel the nerd.'

'And call the Casanova one Max. I always think that's such a suave name and no doubt your Casanova sub-personality is very suave.'

Ollie frowned. 'OK, or maybe just plain Casanova and then there's no confusion. But . . . hhhmm. I might be giving away too much of myself here. Letting you know all my secrets. Come on, then. What about you? Tell me some of yours before I tell you any more of mine.'

'OK. I also have about eight so far. "Obedient Daughter". My mum and dad are pretty strict so I guess I'm a bit of a goodie-two-shoes type when I'm at home, you know, to keep the peace . . .'

'What's her name?'

'Just that: Goody Two Shoes. It used to be on my e-mail address.'

'Used to be? What is it now?'

'Er ... oh, I can't remember.' I felt embarrassed to tell him in case he thought I was a bighead.

'Oh, come on. Mine is superstud@fastmail.org.'

I laughed. 'OK. My mates made me change it. So now it's Babe With Brains.'

Ollie gave me a long look. 'Suits you,' he said.

I felt myself getting hot around the back of my neck. It was very unsettling when he looked at me like that. Made my stomach lurch, but not in an unpleasant way.

'With my mates, I reckon I'm just TJ,' I continued. 'I think I'm the most myself with them ... Um, but I play football and can be a demon on the pitch if I want to be. I'm also arm-wrestling champion. So there's her, the sporty one, Awesome-Arm Annie. Who else? There's the bookworm part of me who reads a lot, but she's probably the same as Goody Two Shoes.'

'What about with boys? Are you the female equivalent of Casanova?'

I burst out laughing. '*Me?* Oh no. No *way*. I turn into Noola the alien girl if ever I see a boy I fancy. My brain turns to mush and I talk gibberish.'

He laughed. 'Noola, huh?'

I couldn't believe that I'd told him about Noola and it was only the second time we'd met. I always thought people would think I was mad, but then Ollie had read Leila's book *and* come up with a whole crowd of his own personalities. If I was mad, so was he.

Ollie stuck out his bottom lip and pouted. 'So that means you don't fancy me. You're talking to me pretty normally.' He reached out and put his hand over mine. 'Noola, Noola don't you like me?'

I laughed. 'Niwingee, blerggghhhh, ehweh . . . See, that's what she sounds like. Like an alien on helium. Nihih. Ug.'

Ollie grinned. 'She *likes* me. Noola likes me. Thank God! So who else is in there?'

I decided not to tell him about the next one I'd put on my list. I called her Lola. She's the girl who came out when I was with Luke de Biasi. Passionate. Romantic. I didn't want to tell Ollie about her in case he asked when I'd discovered her.

'I can't tell you all of them,' I said. 'As then you would know everything about me and so I'd have to kill you, and that would be a shame seeing as we've only just met.'

Ollie laughed. 'I'm glad I came tonight. It's been good seeing you again.'

'Nihih. Ug,' I said, and he grinned even more.

'Noola's back,' he said.

When we left the café, it was still drizzling so we ducked into a shop entrance where I called Mum on my mobile and Ollie called a cab to take him back to his school. As we waited, I wondered if he would try to kiss me or not.

I didn't have to wonder for long.

I was looking in the shop window at the display of shoes when he put his arms round my waist and then turned me to face him. Then he pulled me close and nuzzled into my neck.

'Your hair smells nice,' he murmured. 'Clean. Like apples.'

'Unuh . . . apple shampoo.'

Then he nibbled on my ear lobe. It felt delicious. He turned my face up to his and gave me a kiss. Not a long one, but not short either. It was nice, gentle. He pulled away and I opened my eyes to look at him. He pulled me close again and this time gave me a deeper kiss. I felt my toes curl up and then had a sudden panic. What if Mum drove up and saw us? She'd have a fit if she caught me snogging my face off in the middle of Muswell Hill.

I pulled back. 'Er . . . Mum . . . er, be here . . .'

'No prob,' he said, and reached down and held my hand. 'And hello Goody Two Shoes. Nice to meet you. Can't have Mum catch you mid-snog. And on a school night too!'

I laughed. He was right. Goody Two Shoes had taken over. I hoped he didn't think I was acting childishly or anything. But he was still holding my hand so maybe he didn't mind too much.

'So which of your sub-personalities kissed me?' I asked.

'All of them. They all fancy you!'

I laughed. 'Kissed by eight guys all at the same time. Now that has to be a record. But hey, I don't know all of them yet.'

'Next time,' he said. 'That is, can we do this again?'

'Sure,' I said. I remembered what Nesta had said about there being a time to be cool and a time to say, "Hello sailor, mine's a Diet Coke". This wasn't the time to be cool.

'Maybe Saturday?' asked Ollie.

'Oh. Can't. I'm going to be decorating . . .' I started to say then began to laugh, 'but please don't feel that you have to read a book about interior design and come along and help.'

He laughed too. 'But that's just what I had in mind. I like surprising girls.'

Hmm, I thought. He likes surprising girls. Does that mean that he does this sort of thing a lot?

Just at that moment, his cab drew up and honked.

'I'll call you Saturday,' he said. 'And maybe we can find some more characters lurking within.'

'Deal,' I said, although secretly I thought no way was I telling him about all the people that live in my head. I'd never see him again if I revealed how mad I really am.

Amazing, I thought, as I watched him drive off in the taxi. A date with Ollie Axford. Me. And I've been kissed by him. And all his sub-personalities. It had been a great evening and we'd had a real laugh. He could probably have anyone, I thought. I wonder what on earth he sees in me.

## TJ's Sub-personalities (SPs)

Goody Two Shoes: good girl, does her homework, is punctual, sensible and polite.

Awesome-Arm Annie, the Female Wrestler: football and arm-wrestling champion, a fighter, tomboy, swears like a trooper and will take anyone on.

Noola the Alien: the brainless dribbler I become when I meet cute boys – but she's appearing less often.

Lola: likes all the girlie stuff, perfume, a bit of make-up and boys. Loves Luke de Biasi.

Alice (after Alice in Wonderland): endlessly curious, likes to read about other people's lives and experiences in books, also likes to write, to go to galleries and exhibitions and experience everything that life can offer.

Beryl the Bag Lady: I like to be her on the weekend and slob around in old tracksuits with no make-up. Nesta has a fit if I become Beryl when she's around. Probably not one to mention to Ollie as I know that she's not my most attractive self.

Cassandra, the Prophetess of Doom: miserable old cow who lives at the back of my head. Always moaning – you'll never make it as a writer, you're not good enough, no boy will ever fancy you, you're too boring, you haven't got what it takes, loser. (I'd like to shoot Cassandra, but seeing as she is part of me, that's probably not a very good idea.)

Minnie the Mouse: very timid, hates confrontation and will run away and hide rather than face up to an argument or a difficult situation.

Sometimes one of the sub-personalities is more predominant, and sometimes they all talk at the same time. And debate things. And argue. It can get very tiresome having so many people living in my head.

# Chapter 3

# Kiss Rating

'Out of ten?' asked Nesta the next morning after I'd told the girls about my unexpected evening with Ollie. Of course they wanted all the details right down to how he rated as a kisser.

'Nine and a half,' I replied as we hurried along the corridor into school assembly with a swarm of other chattering girls. 'It was lovely but . . .'

'But what?' asked Izzie. 'Onion breath? Mouth too closed? Too open? Tongue like a wet fish? Teeth like piano keys?'

'Errghh, Izzie,' said Lucy. 'Who have you been kissing lately?'

'No one,' she groaned. 'That's why I can't remember a good kiss.'

'It wasn't like any of that,' I said. 'I don't know. It was lovely, but . . . it was as if he'd read how to do it right, you know? Or like he'd had a lot of practice. It was nice, though. I'm not complaining.'

'I know what you mean,' said Nesta. 'I've been kissed by boys like that. Little bit textbook. Like kissing by numbers. What you really want is someone to be so overwhelmed by their attraction to you they just seize you and go for it but without suffocating you or banging noses . . .'

'You mean like William did that day he kissed you for the first time?' asked Lucy. 'We all saw you. It was *très passionata*.'

'*Très* is French and *passionata* is Italian,' said Izzie, in an attempt to copy our language teacher's posh voice. 'At least, I think it is, so you are mixing your languages, young lady.'

'So?' said Lucy. 'It shows that I am multilingual.'

'Yeah, but I don't think you're meant to speak them all in the same sentence,' said Izzie.

'Says who?' said Lucy. 'Anyway, I like to be different.'

*Très passionata. Muchos fabos.* That was how Luke kissed me and I kissed him back on the one and only time that we snogged, I thought, though I didn't say that to the girls. I didn't want to let on how much I still thought about him. Kissing him had been like melting into a huge vat of marshmallow and chocolate. Perfect. Perfect.

We took our places in our class line-up in the hall and everyone fell silent as Mrs Allen, our headmistress, stood up and began the announcements. Shame we don't do lessons on the art of snogging – it would be very useful, I thought, as Mrs Allen droned on, and I imagined a new timetable: art, history and snog technique. Preferably being taught by members of our favourite boy band, brought in especially for the day. Now that would be an education.

'So can you take me to Homebase?' I asked Mum when I got

in from school. She was in the kitchen, stirring a pan of soup on the stove. The aroma of onions and garlic filled the air.

She shook her head. 'I've got to go back to the surgery after I've done this,' she said as she indicated the soup. 'Dr Plewes has some virus thing so I said I'd do her evening shift for her. Can't it wait until tomorrow after school?'

'Got a meeting for the mag,' I said. (I work as editor for our school magazine, *For Real*, along with Emma Ford from Year Eleven.)

'Saturday morning?'

'That's when I was hoping to start. See, Nesta, Lucy and Izzie have promised that they would come over first thing and I said that I'd have the paint by then. And I've got footie practice in the afternoon. What's Dad doing? Is he home yet?'

Mum jerked her chin towards the living room. 'He's having a snooze,' she said. 'Wasn't feeling too great when he got in. Might be a touch of hayfever at this time of year. I've had a lot of people coming in complaining of it and it can make some people feel quite poorly. He doesn't feel like much supper, so I thought I'd do something light like chicken soup.'

I went through to where Dad was sitting in his armchair with his eyes closed, listening to some piano concerto on a classical music station on the radio.

I went over to him and put my hand on his arm. 'Hey Dad . . .'

'Umph . . .' he started as he awoke. 'Wha . . .?'

'Can you take me to Homebase?'

He rubbed his eyes wearily and glanced at his watch. 'What, now? No. I don't think so.' And he settled into his chair, laid his head back and closed his eyes again.

'Ohhh, Dad, pleeeease . . .'

'Go away. I'm sleeping.'

'But Dad . . . I really need to go now and Mum can't take me and it will only take us half an hour and I won't be able to carry it all on the bus. I know exactly the paint I want and Mum did promise I could do my room and you won't have to do any of the painting because my mates are all going to do that. All you have to do is take me to Homebase and then you can come back and lie in that chair all night and I'll make you a cup of tea and I won't bother you for another moment. I promise.'

Dad opened his eyes and frowned at me. 'God, what a nuisance you are. Like a bee buzzing around in a closed room. Can't a man get even five minutes rest in his own home?'

'Course he can,' I said. 'Only later.' Dad's not as bad-tempered as he sometimes sounds. He likes to stomp about and huff and puff, but underneath it all he's a softie.

He got up and stretched. 'Come on, then. You've woken me up now. Let's get it over with.'

Mum came into the room behind us. 'Are you sure you're all right, Richard?' she asked. 'You're looking a little grey still. How's the head?'

'Well, I was all right,' he said, 'until this nuisance woke me up with her one of her endless demands.'

Mum went over to Dad and put her hand on his forehead. 'I don't know. I think you should maybe go to bed. TJ's paint can wait for another time.'

'Ohhhhhhhhh Muuuuuuuuuuum . . .' I began. 'He said he would . . .'

Dad threw his hands in the air. 'See what I mean? No rest. I'll go to bed when we get back. That's if she's not got another list of things that have to be done right away.'

I grinned up at him. 'Nope. Just the paint. Thanks, Dad. You're a star.'

'I'll wait here and you go and get what you want,' said Dad, and he took a seat in a quiet corner opposite the checkout. Mum had been right, he didn't look too bright, and for a moment I felt my conscience twinge about dragging him out.

'Won't be a mo,' I said. I knew exactly the colours I wanted: Indian sunset, which was a mustard yellow, and Brick Lane, which was a lovely brick red. I'd seen the colour combination in the *Beautiful Homes* magazine that Nesta had brought round and thought it looked fantastic. I'd tried the sample pots of both of them and in all lights, morning and evening, the patches I'd painted looked warm and rich. Once I'd got all my nick-nacks and Indian artefacts in, the overall look was going to be amazing.

I picked out the paints that I needed and took them back to Dad. He got out his wallet and handed me a twenty pound note. 'You go and pay,' he said. 'I'll wait for you here.'

'Oh . . . Um. It's a bit more than that,' I said.

'How much?' said Dad, rooting round in his pocket. 'I've got some spare change in here somewhere.'

I took the seat next to him for a moment. 'Dad, this isn't any old paint. It's made by a company who specialise in recreating colours from old buildings and dynasties in the past. They're designed to have depth on the walls and capture the changing light.'

Dad snorted with laughter. 'Oh, for heaven's sake, TJ, you sound like an advert. Don't be so gullible. I'd have thought you'd have known better than to fall for tosh like that. Depth. Dynasties. Rubbish. Paint is paint. Designer paint? Whatever next?' He pointed at a stand displaying a special offer on huge tubs of white emulsion. 'Look over there. Get some of that. A lick of that will brighten your room and you'll have money to spare.'

'But, Dad, you don't understand. I'm going for a particular look . . .'

Dad rolled his eyes. 'And what, pray, is that?'

'Eastern. All the spice colours that they use in places like India, Thailand . . .'

'And what would you want to paint your room in spice colours for? Because you've been taken in by some silly promotion that says that this is the next best thing, the trend, the fashion . . .'

Oh here we go, I thought, lecture time. Dad likes nothing better than to get on his high horse sometimes and let everyone know exactly what he thinks about the state of the world.

'I'd have thought a girl with your intelligence would have seen through all of that. Nope. Plain white. Can't go wrong with it. And it's cheap.'

I sighed. 'Look, Dad, I haven't been taken in by anything and I don't want my room to look all white and clinical like a hospital ward. And it's not really designer paint, well, not exactly. You're just out of touch with what it all costs. Interiors and gardens are what people are into these days. Making their home space the best they can. And I've done my homework. I've been experimenting with sample pots and the colours I've chosen really do look good. You'll see. But if you really think it's all too expensive then I'll pay you back half out of my next few weeks' pocket money.'

Dad wasn't really listening. 'Waste of money . . .' he grunted. I had to make him understand.

'No, Dad, it's not a waste of money. This is really important to me. You don't realise sometimes how embarrassing it is when people come over to our house. It's like . . . so last century . . .'

Wrong thing to say.

'If you are spending time with people who judge a person by such trivialities as what colour their bedroom is, then I pity you, Theresa Watts.'

'No. They're not like that. Don't judge them. You don't understand. Oh . . . sometimes I wish . . . I wish I had a different father. One who understood or at least *tried* to!'

'Theresa!' said Dad. 'Don't you speak to me like that. You'll be sent straight to your room when we get back and no seeing those friends of yours for a week.'

But it was as if a dam had burst inside of me and I couldn't stop the torrent that came out. I felt like he was treating me like an eight-year-old. 'But it's true. And you're so unwelcoming. I hate having mates over when you're in. I can't enjoy it for fear that you're going to blast through the door at any moment and make me look like an idiot by turfing them out, or telling them to keep the noise down like we're a bunch of kids. Ever wondered why my mates don't hang out much at our house and we always go somewhere else? It's because of *you* . . .' I suddenly got a feeling that I might have gone too far. I glanced up at him.

He didn't look angry. Even worse. He looked disappointed. Or tired. He got out a twenty pound note and a ten pound note and waved them at me, then got up wearily. 'Here. Go on. Take it. I can't be bothered arguing. You go and pay. Take the car keys and I'll meet you at the car. I've just remembered a few things I need to get while I'm here. Light bulbs . . .'

I took the money and the keys, went to the till and paid for my purchases. Even with the amount he'd given me, I had to add what I had left of my pocket money to meet the cost. I felt cross with Dad. He can be such a stick in the mud sometimes. Cantankerous old bugger, I thought, as I put the paint in a bag and went out to the car. I was wrong at home earlier when I'd thought that he has a soft centre. He hasn't. He's just gone rotten inside.

Once I'd slammed the boot shut on the paint, sat down in the passenger seat and taken some deep breaths, I calmed down. Oops, I thought. Might have pushed my luck a bit there. I'm usually Goody Two Shoes with Dad. It's the easiest way to be, but some other sub-personality had escaped and had her say. One with a very big mouth! I'll have to think about giving her a name . . . Nesta. I laughed to myself, as she's usually the one out of all of us who speaks before she thinks. I could call my inner-loud mouth Nesta mark two.

As I sat waiting in the car, I began to feel guilty about my outburst. Dad's not so bad, really. Just a bit grumpy sometimes. Maybe I am too. Like father, like daughter. I decided that I would apologise when he got back to the car and make him a special tea tray with the ginger biscuits he likes when we got home.

Dad seemed to be taking ages, so I listened to the car radio for a while then continued concocting an apology in my head. After a while, my mobile rang.

'Hello,' said a male voice.

'Hello,' I said.

'Who am I talking to?'

I recognised the voice as Ollie's. 'I'm not sure,' I said. 'I think I've just met a new character in my head. A very stroppy one.'

'What's her name?'

'Nest . . . no . . . I'll call her Susie the strop queen, I think. Yeah. That fits. Who am I talking to?'

'Er . . . Jock,' he replied. 'I've just finished a squash match so I guess it's my sporty persona that's predominant. Hey, do you think that if Jock had a surname, it would be Strap?'

'Good one,' I said. 'I used to collect mad names and the books they'd written, like Chest Complaints by Ivor Tickliecoff. That sort of thing. Drink Problems by Imorf Mihead. Run to the Loo by Willie Makeit.'

Ollie cracked up laughing. 'Hey, did you e-mail Leila your question?'

'Yes, but she hasn't answered yet.'

'Where are you? I can hear traffic in the background. Sirens.'

'Yeah,' I said as the sirens got louder and an ambulance whizzed past. 'I'm in the carpark at Homebase, waiting for Dad.'

'Sounds like you're in the middle of Piccadilly Circus.'

I turned to see what was going on and saw that the ambulance had stopped at the entrance. Men had got out of the back and were rushing into the store with a stretcher. 'Guess someone's taken ill,' I said. 'It's like *ER* and they're going in.'

'You said your dad is a doctor, didn't you?' asked Ollie.

'Yeah.'

'So maybe he's in there doing mouth to mouth and that thumping the chest thing they do . . .'

'Yeah. Knowing Dad, he'll be supervising everybody. I'd better go and haul him out or we'll be here all night. Look, I'll call you later, hey?'

'Oh . . . OK.'

I cut Ollie off as I'd suddenly had a strange feeling that something was wrong. I got out of the car and ran back into the store to find Dad. To the right of the till, I could see the ambulance men bent over someone on a stretcher, giving them oxygen. I glanced at the people around. No sign of Dad. Maybe he hadn't got involved after all.

I ran up and down a few aisles to see where he'd got to. Light bulbs, he'd said, but there was no sign of him in the electrical department. A cold shiver ran down my spine.

Oh God, I thought, as I raced back to the front of the store. The paramedics were rushing to get someone into the ambulance. They looked very worried.

I chased after them to see who was on the stretcher, but the man carrying the rear part of it blocked my view.

I could see the patient's shoes clear enough, though.

Expensive looking.

Black brogues.

Dad's.

# Chapter 4

# Dear God, This is TJ

**Waiting for Mum** to arrive at the hospital.

Waiting for the doctors to tell me something. Anything.

Waiting. Waiting. Waiting as people in white coats rushed in and out of the room where they'd taken Dad. A young doctor introduced himself as Dr Miller and asked me to wait outside. He directed me to a corner where there were four rows of orange plastic chairs.

I didn't like the smell of the place, a mix between disinfectant and boiled vegetables. Not nice. I sat there for a while and tried to distract myself by looking through one of last year's magazines that were in a well worn pile on the window ledge, but I couldn't concentrate. The words seemed to swim in front of me. I wanted to phone my mates but I knew that mobiles aren't allowed to be used in hospitals, and I didn't want to go outside in case Mum arrived or Dr Miller came out. I thought about texting, but I wasn't sure if that was allowed either and didn't want to risk it. It would be too awful if I used my phone and it interfered with someone's life support machine and they died as a result and then I'd be responsible for killing *two* people in here. I could have used the public phone at the end of the corridor, but I hadn't got any change left. I'd spent it all on that stupid paint. All thoughts of decorating my room seemed a million miles away now. Irrelevant. A stupid idea. If it wasn't for me pushing Dad to take me to Homebase, this might not have happened. Who would want a gorgeous bedroom and no dad? Oh God, I hope he's OK, I thought for the hundredth time. I soooo wish I hadn't said all those terrible things to him.

I remembered a poem that we did in school that starts: *Time is too slow for those that wait.* Tell me about it, I thought, as I got up and paced the corridor. I can't stay here, I'm going mad, I decided, and set off for the escalator and down to the entrance on the ground floor to look for Mum.

An assortment of people flowed in and out the automatic doors. All ages. A bald man on crutches, a teenage girl with a broken arm, a pregnant lady, lots of old people. Outside, I could see people on the grass verge opposite having a sneaky fag and catching the last rays of sun. Inside, people were making enquiries at the information desk, and buying flowers, chocolates, books or magazines at the shop at the back. In and out, in and out people went. It felt unreal. Like a dream. Or nightmare. So many with an urgent look on their face, like me, concerned about a loved one. In a hurry to get somewhere. But where was Mum? Surely she should have been here by now, I thought as I checked my watch. Oh God, please don't let anything have happened to her, too. Maybe I'd missed her and she was going up in the lift when I was going down the escalator.

I raced back up to the first floor, back to the rows of chairs where I'd been told to wait, but she wasn't there. Just empty seats.

Back down the corridor.

Back down the escalator.

My jaw felt so tight. I cursed the fact that Mum didn't have a mobile. No need, they both said. What do we need those newfangled things for, they'd asked. For times like *this*, I thought.

Back to the entrance.

An ambulance flew by and pulled up in the emergency bay. More people coming and going.

Where was Mum?

I was about to call Izzie when at last I saw Mum hurrying across the forecourt. Her face was drawn and anxious. I waved when I saw her and ran out to join her.

She gave me a brief hug as we both walked back inside. 'Oh, TJ. Where is he? A and E?'

I motioned towards the escalator. 'They rushed him through upstairs. First floor. What did they tell you when they called?'

'They didn't really tell me a lot over the phone. Just to get here as quickly as I could,' she said, as we stepped on to the escalator. 'It took me forever to get here, and then the parking – it's a disgrace. I've been driving round and round, and in the end I just had to leave it. Probably get clamped. What's been happening?'

'They haven't told me anything – although when we got here, I think I heard one of them say that he might have had a stroke. What does that mean exactly? Will he be all right?'

Mum took a quick intake of breath. 'I don't know, TJ. Not until I've spoken with the doctors.'

We reached the top of the escalator and stepped off on to the first floor.

'This way,' I said, and led Mum back to where I had been waiting. I showed her the row of chairs. 'They asked me to wait here.'

Mum looked around. It was clear she had no intention of sitting down and waiting. 'Which room is he in?' she asked.

I pointed to the room along the corridor. 'In there. But they wouldn't let me in.'

'You stay here,' she said. 'I'll find out what's happening.'

I sank down on to one of the chairs while Mum charged along the corridor and knocked on the door I'd pointed out to her.

The door opened a crack. I heard hushed voices – Mum's raised – then she disappeared inside.

Once again, I was on my own. Waiting, waiting, waiting.

My imagination went into an overdrive of scary scenarios: the doctors coming out and saying it was all over, nothing they could do. A funeral, Marie, Paul, Mum and I in black. A headstone saying R. Watts. Mum sleeping alone in their big, wide bed, their wardrobe of clothes, his side empty . . .

Stop it, I told myself, *stop* it, stop it. I could hardly breathe. He'll be all right. He's my dad. He's always all right.

To stop myself thinking black thoughts, I got up and went into the Ladies by the escalator. I felt like crying and I felt like kicking something, both at the same time. Angry, mad, sad. I kicked the tiled wall by the sink.

'Owwwwww!' I cried, as bone met tile. It felt like I'd broken my toe.

I went and sat in a cubicle, reached for a tissue but no tears would come. I felt so alone and helpless and never more in need of my friends. Should I go outside and call Izzie, Lucy or Nesta, I asked myself. What could they say? What would I tell them? Plus, I didn't want to wander too far in case Mum came out again. I still felt numb with disbelief that this could be happening. For the millionth squillionth time that evening, I played over in my head the argument I'd had with Dad in Homebase. Why had I said such terrible things? That I wished I had a different father. That I hated having my mates over when he was home. Awful things. I must have really hurt him. I hoped he knew I didn't mean it. I wish I could tell Mum what I'd said and she could pat my hand and say, Oh TJ, you didn't mean that, like she'd done a thousand times when I'd been letting off steam about him after he'd been grumpy. But he'd never had a stroke before. Was what I'd said the last straw for him? Was I to blame? I so wished I could talk to someone about it, one of my mates or Marie or Paul, but I didn't know if I could bear to see or hear their reaction when I told them what I'd said. They'd try and cover it, but inside they'd be thinking, What a mean girl. All the things I was thinking myself.

I felt so ashamed. If people knew what I was really like, I thought, they'd hate me. Hannah would have understood. I thought about going outside and texting her, but decided against it until I had a clearer idea of what was happening. I didn't want to freak her out. I still missed her. We often used to have a moan about our dads as hers was a headmaster and very strict with her. Funnily enough, though, she'd always got on with my dad and could say cheeky things to him that I'd never have got away with in a million years. But that was Hannah. She was so totally bonkers that everybody loved her, even my dad.

I got up, went over to the window and looked out at the evening sky.

How could it all have happened so quickly? One moment you're shopping for paint, and the next your whole life might be altered for ever. My chest tightened with fear.

'Dear God, this is TJ. If you're up there, please, *please* let my dad live. Please don't let what I said to him be the last words between us,' I said to the sky.

Why am I talking to the sky? I wondered. Why would God be up there? They've sent rockets up far enough and they've never come back with any evidence of anything along those lines. There's a sun and stars up there, other solar systems too, but no God and angels. And even if there was, how was he going to hear me from such a long way away. I decided to give it another go anyway.

'Oh God. *Are* you there? *Is* anybody listening?'

If there is anyone out there, I thought, why should he listen to *me*? I'm in a hospital full of sick people and probably all their relatives and friends are praying, at this very moment, leaning out of the windows in the toilets dotted around the hospital on every floor. Please God help us, please God help my dad, my mum, my sister, daughter, son, brother, friend. Over and over again. But people get sick. And die. So if there is a God, why should he, she or it help *me*? Horrible me with the mean tongue. I wished Izzie was here. She thinks a lot about God and life and death and stuff. She might know who to pray to and what to say. If anyone had a hotline to anybody up there, it would be Iz.

I blew my nose and decided to go down and out into the forecourt to call her or Nesta or Lucy, but just as I stepped back into the corridor, I saw Mum come out of Dad's room and look round for me. Her face was as white as the walls and as I raced down to join her, a thought flashed through my mind that Dad must have been mad to have suggested that I paint my room at home that colour. Such a reminder of illness and hospitals and doctors and worry. I'd have thought he'd have wanted to get away from it and flood his life outside with the brightest colours imaginable.

'How is he?' I asked.

Mum sat down heavily on one of the plastic chairs. She looked worn out. 'They've confirmed that he's had a stroke,' she said. 'They're doing tests.'

'What does having a stroke mean, exactly? Will he get better?'

'TJ, stop asking that. We don't know,' snapped Mum, then took a deep breath. 'No one knows at this stage. It depends how bad it was. Some people make full recoveries. Others don't. It's too early to tell, really.' She reached out and put her hand over mine. 'One thing we do know, though, and that is he's a tough old bird.'

'Worst case scenario,' I said. This was a term I'd heard Mum use when talking to Dad about her patients. I knew she'd understand what I wanted to know.

'Worst case? Hopefully it won't come to worst case. Your father's been an active man . . .'

'Mum, I want to know. Nothing could be worse than what I've been sitting here imagining.'

'I don't want to alarm you, TJ. It's too early to say anything for certain.' She patted my knee. 'One of us ought to give Marie and Paul an update. They'll be worried as I let them know that Dad had been brought here before I left home. I'll go and call them, then I'm going back in with your dad for a while. Why don't you go and get both of us something to drink from that shop downstairs while I go and make the calls? I'm parched.'

I stood up and my legs felt wobbly, like someone had taken the bones out. I made myself take a deep breath. I have to keep it together, I thought, for Mum and for Dad. 'OK. And Dad? Would he like anything? Shall I get him a cup of tea?'

Mum's eyes misted over and she took my hand again. 'Not at the moment, love. He's not quite up to cups of tea yet. Maybe later.'

Seeing Mum's eyes fill with tears made my eyes water, too. Up until then, I'd felt too numb. Not sure of what was going on. But seeing Mum's reaction, I now knew.

It was really serious.

And it was all my fault.

> *Time is too slow for those who wait,*
> *Too swift for those who fear,*
> *Too long for those who grieve,*
> *Too short for those who rejoice,*
> *But for those who love, time is eternity.*
>
> Henry Van Dyke (1852 –1933)

# Chapter 5

# Guru Schmuru

'Don't ask me,' groaned Izzie, as we walked out arm in arm to the playground at lunch the following day. 'I don't know . . .'

'But you're always reading books about God and different religions and meditating . . .' I said as we took up our positions on a bench, ready to take advantage of the early summer sun that we'd been having lately.

'That's because I'm looking for answers. And I'm looking for answers because I don't have any,' said Izzie.

Tell me about it, I thought. I had so many questions, and it felt weird to be at school when I knew that Dad was in the hospital and still in a serious condition. I wanted to be there with him. I was desperate to know that he was all right and then, when it was appropriate, to apologise for the awful things that I had said. I'd called Izzie, Lucy and Nesta when I'd got home and we'd talked for ages on the phone about what had happened. I told them everything and not one of them made me feel bad about what I'd said. All of them said over and over again that it wasn't my fault. Izzie even offered to come over and sleep at my house, but I told her not to as it was so late. I didn't sleep a wink – I kept thinking about Dad and felt exhausted when it was time to get up and go to school. Marie and Paul were at the hospital as they'd both driven through the night when they'd heard the news (Marie from Devon and Paul from Bristol), but Mum had insisted that I went to school and tried to carry on as normal. Normal. Hah! I couldn't concentrate on anything. I felt like my brain was full of bubbles and my stomach full of knots.

Lucy, Izzie and Nesta did their best to comfort me, waiting at the gates for me with hugs and sympathy. I could feel them watching me every minute through morning classes, but even their kindness couldn't take away the fear and shame I felt inside.

'Do you want anything?' asked Nesta. 'Drink? Sandwich? Naked boy to dance in front of you to take your mind off things?'

The image of a naked boy prancing about the playground being chased by Miss Watkins did make me laugh for a moment but I shook my head.

'No thanks. I'm off naked boys this week. Maybe next week. You can bring in a coach-load of them then.'

'Sure,' said Nesta, squeezing my arm, then reaching into her bag and getting out her tiny lip-gloss tin. 'Here. Use this. You don't want your lips to get dry in the sun. And let me know if you change your mind about the dancing boys.'

I took the lip-gloss and lifted the lid. The familiar scent of Nesta's strawberry gloss was strangely reassuring. I applied a little then passed it on to Izzie. 'I will. To tell you the truth, I'm off boys, period. Ollie phoned me yesterday and then texted later after I got back from the hospital, but I don't even feel like talking to him at the moment.'

'I wish there was something we could do to help,' said Nesta. 'I hate seeing you like this.'

'You can help. You can tell me if there's a God or not,' I said.

Nesta laughed. 'Ah,' she said. 'You might have got me stumped there.'

Lucy got her sunglasses out of her bag, put them on and tilted her head up towards the sun. 'Of course there's a God,' she said. 'Has to be. It's obvious.'

'How?' I asked.

Lucy held up her hands. 'Just look around you. Where did it all come from if there isn't a God?'

'Big bang,' I said. 'Universe expanding. Evolution.'

Lucy shook her head. 'Nah. There has to be an intelligent being behind it all. There are too many fab things to look at. Birds. Fish. Animals. Flowers. That's the proof for me. In the same way that you can't have a painting without a painter, you can't have this creation without a creator.'

'OK, but where?' I asked.

Lucy laughed. 'You mean like his address? I don't know. Although when I was a kid I used to write to God and post my letters in the postbox.'

'Me too,' said Izzie. 'And I always used to put on airmail stickers. I imagined God up in the sky somewhere.'

'Yeah. Why is that?' I asked. 'Why do we talk to the sky?'

Izzie shrugged.

'I used to write to Santa Claus,' I said. 'And address the letters to the North Pole.'

'And then put them by the chimney,' said Lucy. 'We all did.'

Up until then, Nesta had been munching on a peanut butter sandwich and listening. She swallowed her last bite. 'OK, Lucy,' she said. 'I can understand your no creation without a creator bit, yeah, but it's not all beautiful is it? It's not all flowers and birds. Like if God created it *all*, why is there so much pain and war . . .'

'God didn't make that,' said Lucy. 'The human race did. It's not God who makes bombs and guns, it's people.'

'But according to your theory, creator behind creation, etc., then the creator made everything down here. So God made the human race too, yeah?' said Nesta.

Lucy nodded.

'If that's the case,' Nesta continued, 'then he must have known that some humans would have a nasty streak. If your God is so top, Lucy, what about snakes and crocodiles and oh . . . all the things in creation that are horrible . . . If God made them too then he's got a nasty streak.' She batted away a wasp that was flying around near her head. 'And wasps! Explain them! Horrible things.'

'And is God a he, she or it? Which, Lucy?' asked Izzie.

Lucy pushed her glasses down along her nose and peered at us. '*Stop* ganging up on me,' she said. '*I'm* not an expert. I just believe that there is something, that's all, and it makes me feel good to pray sometimes. I can't explain it, but *don't* give *me* a hard time over it. And in answer to your question, Iz, God's a she. Haven't you seen those T-shirts with the slogan, *When God made man, she was only joking?* Makes sense to me.'

'Haven't your books told you *anything*, Iz?' I asked.

Izzie shrugged her shoulders. 'Some say that God isn't so much like the clichéd, white-bearded old bloke, but more like a force or energy . . .'

'Yeah,' said Nesta. 'Makes more sense. Like in *Star Wars* . . . may the Force be with you . . .'

'But we don't know where it is or why it is . . .' I said. 'Freaky when you think about it.'

Nesta got out her sunglasses and laid her head back like Lucy. 'Phew, it's hot!' she said, gesturing at the sky. 'Listen guys, the sun is shining, the sky is blue, we have each other. My philosophy is just get on with life and have a good time while you can. You could drive yourself mad questioning it all.'

'I can't help it,' said Izzie. 'I really want to know why we're here and what for and where we go when we die and where we were before we were born.'

'Just accept that you have a pea brain,' said Nesta. 'Some things are just tooooo darn big for you to understand.'

Izzie playfully thumped her arm. 'Me? A pea brain? Cheek. You're right, though. Looking for answers can drive you mad. The number of times I've asked teachers and my parents. No one's told me anything for sure.'

'Where do people go when they die, Izzie?' I asked.

'Devon,' said Izzie, giggling. 'Remember I told you about that little boy at my stepsister's wedding? He said that prayer. Our Father, who art in heaven . . . only he said Devon. If only it was that easy and you got his address and phone number in the telephone directory, like, Doctor: 142 Baronsmere Road; Plumber: 56 High Street; God: 28 Paradise Close, Devon.'

'I reckon the only way to find out what happens when you die,' said Nesta, 'is to die and find out.'

'There are books on the afterlife,' said Izzie, 'and loads of stuff on the Internet about people who have had near death experiences. Most of them said it was wonderful and took away their fear . . .'

'Yeah, but how do we know it wasn't a dream or wishful thinking?' asked Nesta. 'And all that stuff that's in books, most of it's speculation. We don't *really* know, do we? You know what I think it must be like, dying?'

'What?' I asked.

'Like going to the airport and knowing full well that you're going on a journey, only no luggage allowed. No make-up, no mags or mobile phones. And you don't know the destination.'

'Really, *really* freaky,' I said with a shudder.

'Might be, might not be,' said Nesta. 'Thing is, though, we don't know. None of us. But what we do know is this: here we are *now*. We're mates. Life is OK – most of the time, anyway.' She smiled sympathetically at me. 'So as I said before, stop freaking yourself out thinking about how it might be and enjoy what is.'

'Wow,' said Izzie. 'That is so Zen, Nesta. You know, you're quite wise in your own stupid way.'

Nesta grinned. 'Ta. Just called me Guru Schmuru.'

I looked around at the three of them. Maybe mates are proof that there's some good in the world, I thought. Never mind angels or airy fairy stuff you can't see. I've got the real thing with Izzie, Lucy and Nesta.

'And I don't think it does any harm to pray now and again,' said Lucy. 'In case anyone *is* listening.'

Izzie put her hand on mine. 'You're thinking about all this because of your dad, aren't you?' she asked.

I nodded. 'Sort of. Does make you think, doesn't it? You know, when something like this happens.'

'What did your mum say when you rang at break?' asked Nesta.

'She said he's stable but he's still not able to talk or move much. Mum says he knows she's there, though. She told him to blink if he understood what she was saying, and he blinked five times.'

'He'll be OK,' said Nesta. 'He's Scary Dad. He won't go down without a fight.'

I wished I could be as sure as she sounded. And I wished that I could believe that there was a God who listened the way that Lucy believed. I decided to put my uncertainty aside and pray anyway. I had nothing to lose, so each night I prayed that Dad would recover fully, that I'd get a chance to apologise and that he'd be able to come home soon. I wasn't sure if anyone or anything was listening, but somehow it made me feel better to talk through my thoughts, hopes and fears out loud.

Every day we visited the hospital and each day there wasn't much change. I was allowed in to see Dad, but I wasn't sure he even knew that I was there, even though he did blink in reply when I asked questions. Most of the time he looked like he was asleep, and it was horrible seeing him strapped to all sorts of machines. I so wanted to apologise to him, but wasn't sure he would hear me.

There was talk of a convalescent home.

Talk of physiotherapists.

Talk of wonder drugs.

But nobody really knew how things were going to develop. It was awful seeing Mum around the house. She was so quiet and looked so strained, and I realised how dependent Dad and she were on each other. I was reliant on my mates and hadn't even known them that long. Dad had been Mum's companion for almost forty years, and without him grumping about the place she seemed lost and didn't know what to do with herself.

She went into work as normal, saying that there was no point in her sitting around moping and that she still had her own patients to see. Marie fussed about cleaning, cooking and insisting that we all ate properly to keep our strength up. I think it gave her something to do, although the endless scones and quiches she made inevitably got binned as no one had much appetite. Paul mainly occupied himself by lying on the sofa watching hours of daytime telly. Mum would normally have told him 'to get off his backside and do something useful' but she didn't tell him off once. She didn't say anything about Mojo sleeping on the end of my bed every night either. Even he seemed to have picked up on the fact that something was wrong and was being especially attentive to me.

The atmosphere in the house was so subdued that I was grateful that the girls insisted that I spent time at their houses whenever I wasn't at school or the hospital. They were my strawberry-scented guardian angels, always on hand at break and lunch with chocolate, lip-gloss, magazines and chat to try and take my mind off things. They seemed to understand that I wasn't in the mood for talking a lot so we'd just hang out, reading magazines or soaking up the sun.

Ollie e-mailed but I didn't feel like answering. He also texted a couple of times. I let him know that Dad was ill so he didn't think that I was rude not replying, but when he texted back again I sent a message that I'd be in touch properly when things were better. In my experience, boys upset the balance and my balance was upset enough as it was at the moment.

Five days after Dad had been in the hospital, Mum got a call saying that he was showing signs of coming round fully. We raced to the hospital and there he was sitting up a little and looking very grumpy. He was still weak, but he could clearly see and he could definitely hear and talk and feel.

I'd never felt so relieved in my life.

'We'll have him back up and about in no time,' said Dr Miller. 'He's doing well.'

'Hrumph,' groaned Dad. 'Call this doing well? Your eyesight needs testing, man.'

After that his recovery was swift, and it wasn't long before Dad was back in his Scary Dad persona: ordering the nurses around, telling the doctors what to do, moaning about the food, being woken up too early, the noise, the hard bed, lumpy pillows and the man in the room next door who was snoring.

I was so happy to hear him and grinned every time he opened his mouth to complain. It meant Dad was back. He was getting better.

'A change of lifestyle,' said Dr Rolland, one of Dad's doctor friends who was over one evening for a visit. 'That's what you need, Richard. Take a break.'

'I will, I will,' said Dad. 'Just get me out of this place.'

'All in good time,' said Dr Rolland. 'Just a couple more days, but don't even think of getting back to your normal routine. Time off is what you need.'

Dad pulled a face and, for a moment, looked like a naughty schoolboy, but he nodded. 'Don't worry,' he said. 'I'm not an idiot.'

'Didn't say you were,' said Dr Rolland, 'but if you don't take heed of what your body's telling you, you will be.'

As a further sign that Dad was recovering, Marie and Paul went back to their respective homes. The night after they'd gone, I finally got some time alone with him.

'Um . . . Dad?'

'Yes?'

'About . . . well . . . about what happened . . . you know . . . at Homebase?'

Dad nodded.

'Yes. But before that, I . . . I said some awful things and I want you to know . . .' I felt a lump come into my throat and I didn't think I was going to be able to get the words out. 'I . . . I want you to know that I'm truly sorry and I didn't mean what I said and I do love . . .'

Dad put his hand over mine. 'Forgotten, TJ,' he said. 'We all say things in the heat of the moment, but you and I know what we really feel about each other, don't we?'

Tears pricked my eyes and Dad looked at me with such tenderness.

'Hey, hey,' he said and squeezed my hand. 'No need for the waterworks.'

I leaned over the bed and rested my head on his chest. 'I'm *so* glad you didn't die, Dad.'

'Me too, TJ,' he said softly. 'Me too.'

When God made man, she was only joking.

# Chapter 6

# Sweaty Betty

'Where are you off to?' asked Mum, the Thursday evening after we'd got back from the hospital. It was exactly one week since Dad had collapsed, but it felt like a lifetime.

'For a run,' I said, as I laced up my trainers and headed for the front door.

Mum gave me a quizzical look. 'But you're wearing make-up.'

'Never know who you might bump into,' I said, and waved. 'Back soon.'

I took off down our road and jogged over towards Cherry Tree Woods. I felt the need to work off some of the pent-up feelings and energy after the rollercoaster week with Dad. There was a light rain, but the evening was warm and it felt good to be out in the fresh, fragrant air after so many evenings cooped up in the hospital room with its airless, claustrophobic atmosphere. All the front gardens were beginning to flower –

pink montana and roses of every variety tumbled over porches, and pergolas, yellow laburnum and lilac trees dripped flowers over fences, while rhododendrons and azaleas budded in corners. I knew all the names because Mum'd taught me them when we used to go for walks when I was little.

I got to the park and, after once round, still felt I could go further so I ran towards Highgate and down to the Archway Road. As far as Biasi's, then I'd turn back, I thought. Biasi's was the restaurant owned by Luke's parents. He worked in there sometimes and, as I ran towards it and it came into view, I had an idea. I'd get a takeaway for Dad for his lunch tomorrow. Mum could take it in for him. He loved good Italian food and had complained non-stop about the hospital food since he'd been in there. I could go into Biasi's and get him something. I had a ten pound note in my pocket so it should be enough. He'd love it. I slowed my speed down so that when I arrived there, if by any chance Luke was working, I wouldn't look like a pink sweaty Betty.

There were only a few customers at tables when I pushed the door open and made my way over to the bar area, where a middle-aged man was talking to Mrs Biasi. She looked as glamorous as ever, in a low-cut red top showing off her ample cleavage. I didn't expect that she'd remember me as I'd only been in there once with Nesta and the others. It didn't matter. She seemed to treat everyone like they were her long lost friend.

'Eat, enjoy,' she was saying to the man as she handed him a takeaway carton. 'And come back soon, it's always good to see you, and bring that lovely wife of yours.'

I waited until she had finished, then took a step forward.

'Er . . . I wonder if you can help me. I want to order some food for my dad. He's in hospital so I thought my mum could take it to him for lunch tomorrow . . .'

Mrs Biasi's expression became concerned. 'Oh, your papa's not good, so sad,' she said.

'He'll be OK, I think. Just he hates the hospital food . . .'

'Understandable,' said Mrs Biasi, and she made a face like she had a bad smell under her nose. 'It not good.'

'So something light and fresh, I thought.'

'You good girl. You think right. We fix him something very nice in the kitchen. I have just the thing for him. You wait here. Eat olives,' she said as she thrust a bowl towards me then disappeared into the back. I popped an olive into my mouth. It was delicious. Then I looked around for Luke. There was no sign of him; only one Italian-looking girl serving the waiting customers. It felt strange to be on Luke's territory: exciting in one way as I knew that he might walk in at any moment, and scary in another as I wasn't sure how I'd react. Or how he would. It had been months since I'd seen him and the sharpness of his features had begun to dim in my mind. Was he really as gorgeous as I remembered? Would I feel the same about him? Now that I had met Ollie, I wanted to know if those feelings for Luke were still there.

Mrs Biasi came back about ten minutes later and handed me a bag that smelled of herbs and garlic. 'Your father will enjoy this,' she said. 'Made with fresh pesto and sundried tomatoes. Very good. My own recipe. Now you make sure you come back if he'd like some more. Good food and sleep, that's what he needs. Tell him to rest. Not get up too soon.'

I had to laugh. She had never met him and here she was saying what he needed. I paid her for the food and was about to leave when I found myself turning back.

'Er . . . I . . . is Luke around?'

Mrs Biasi gave me a penetrating look. 'Luke? Ah. You're a friend of Luke's?'

'Er . . . sort of . . .' No need to explain that actually we weren't friends, I thought, or that I was Nesta's friend and had almost stolen her boyfriend. No need for details.

'He's at class tonight,' she said. 'Acting class.'

'Oh, right. Yes,' I said. 'Sorry. Thank you.'

'What's your name? Shall I tell him you called?'

I could feel myself blushing. I started to back away. 'Oh. No. Thanks. I'll come again.'

Mrs Biasi looked amused. I bet she'd seen a hundred bashful girls come in and ask for her son over the years.

'OK. Right. Bye then,' I said and left as fast as I could.

I felt disappointed as I walked up the street. Deflated. And I felt tired and no longer in the mood for running home. I crossed the road and went to stand at the bus stop where, luckily, I didn't have to wait long as already I could see a bus lumbering up the hill. It drew up at the stop and the doors opened. I stood aside to let the passengers off. Out of the corner of my eye I saw a tall guy get off and head down the hill then swing back.

'TJ? TJ Watts?'

I glanced up and my heart almost stopped.

It was Luke.

'Oh. Ah . . .' I said as I stood frozen to the spot.

'You getting on or going to stop there all day?' called the bus driver when everyone was aboard.

'Er . . . I . . .'

Luke pulled me into a bear hug. 'She'll catch a later bus,' he said.

'Ohmigod!' said Izzie later that night. 'And then what happened? Eyes met. Stomachs lurched. Arms touched. I can hardly take the suspense. Then what?'

I'd called Izzie immediately after getting home. It wasn't that I didn't want to tell Lucy or Nesta about seeing Luke, it was just that Izzie had been so supportive of me through the whole painful saga with him before Christmas. I knew that she'd listen without jumping to conclusions or judging me in any way. Even though I loved all three of my mates, I sometimes felt that Izzie understood me best.

'We went and had a coffee in a café up the other end of the road to Biasi's. He seemed sooo pleased to see me . . .'

'Coffee? *Coffee?* Didn't he sweep you away to some romantic little spot and confess his undying love to you?'

'No. We went to a burger joint.'

'*Burger* joint? Pff. He's got to work on his romantic locations, TJ.'

'But it was romantic. Anywhere he is feels romantic.'

'Ah. So you still feel the same about him?'

'Yep. Stronger than ever.' Seeing Luke again had been amazing and he was twice as gorgeous as I remembered. Tall with shoulder-length hair, chiselled jaw, wide mouth. With his looks, he was classic Hollywood material. 'I really do, Iz. And seeing him again has only made me more sure that there's something special between us. He has this effect on me that is totally amazing. Like time stands still, like the world is a happy place . . .'

'Eewww. Totally vomitous.' Izzie laughed at the other end of the other end of the phone. 'But I always knew you had it bad for this guy. Did you snog him?'

'No. I wanted to. Boy, did I want to. *Boy*, did I want to. But no. I haven't forgotten how he was two-timing Nesta and I, and God knows who else.'

'So what did you do?'

'We talked.'

'Talked?'

'Yeah. He asked how my writing was going. I asked about his acting classes. Then we talked about our dads. Remember his dad is like mine in that he's way strict. He was actually lovely about Dad, really sympathetic. And he held my hand all the time and stroked my hair. And he was so pleased to see me. He said . . . he said that he'd thought about me a lot and wished that things could have been different and that he was sorry he blew it.'

'Amazing how you just bumped into him like that,' said Izzie. 'Where was it?'

'Well . . . er . . . down near the Archway Road.'

'Isn't that near where his parents' restaurant is?'

'Is it? Oh . . . um yes, it is, isn't it?'

Izzie laughed. 'And you just *happened* to be passing.'

'Yes, actually. It wasn't planned.'

'Yeeaah. Right. Sounds to me that you're in denial about Luke, and I don't mean the river in Egypt.'

'No really, Iz. OK. So I do still fancy him. Yes, the chemistry is very strong, but I hadn't planned to go in and see him . . .'

'Not consciously. But it sounds like your unconscious knew exactly which way it was thinking.'

'So what do I do?'

'I don't know. Do you want to see him again?'

'Yes.'

'But what about Ollie?'

'What about Ollie?' I asked.

'Ollie Axford? Last seen in Muswell Hill snogging your face off. Aren't you going out with him?'

That shut me up for a moment. I hadn't even thought about Ollie.

'TJ, TJ, are you still there?' asked Izzie, as I took a few moments to wonder if I *should* be considering Ollie Axford. The image of him nibbling my ear up in Muswell Hill flashed through my mind. Hmmm. He is cute and fun to be with and now that Dad's getting better maybe I should reply properly to his texts and e-mails.

'Yeah, I'm still here. Thinking about Ollie. It's not exactly as if I'm going out with him. Oh God, I don't know. I like him too. But we're just getting to know each other, really. He's great company but it's not like we're in a relationship.'

'Are you going to see Luke again?'

'He did say that he'd like to and I told him that I'd think about it. It would be OK, wouldn't it? It wouldn't be like I was two-timing either of them.'

Izzie was silent at the other end of the phone.

'Izzie . . . are you still there?'

'Yeah.'

'So what are you thinking?'

'I'm thinking, my dear TJ, that you sound just how Luke must have sounded when he talked about you and Nesta. Liked both of you, etc, etc. Very tempting to see both of you, etc, etc.'

'But I wouldn't do that. He was *dating* Nesta and he told lies,' I said. 'I've been on the other end of that and I know how it feels.'

'So you'll be telling Ollie about Luke then will you? And Luke about Ollie?'

'Yeah. Of course, if it comes up. Oh, I don't know. I like both of them. Why does it have to be like this? Boys, huh? They're like buses. You wait for ages, no sign of any and then along come two. Do I *have* to choose?'

'Some time,' said Izzie.

'But I can't. And it would be mad to tell either of them about the other when it's such early days. They'd be like, er, what's your problem? We're not even dating regularly. Can't I just see both of them and then decide?'

'Yeah. You could,' said Izzie, then she was silent again.

'Holy crapoley,' I said. 'I'm a love rat!'

Denial is not a river in Egypt.

## Chapter 7

# Destiny?

In the end, I decided it wasn't Ollie or Luke that I needed to talk to. I discussed it some more with Izzie and we both agreed that there was someone far more important to tell.

'Hey, Nesta, can I have a word?' I asked when I saw her come through the school gates the next morning. Luckily she was on her own. Izzie and Lucy had already gone in as they wanted to go to the cloakroom before assembly.

'Looks serious. Are you OK? Is your dad OK?'

I nodded. 'He's going to be fine. No, it's . . .'

Now that she was standing in front of me, I felt nervous. Luke had almost broken us up as friends and now here I was about to ask her permission to see him again. No. I couldn't do it. 'Er . . . tell you what, Nesta. It doesn't matter. Temporary loss of insanity. Forget it.'

'Wow. It really is serious. Come on. You can trust me.'

'I know. And that's exactly why I . . . um . . . have changed my mind.'

Nesta began to mock-strangle me. 'Then I vill have to kill you. I hate it when someone begins to say something then holds back on me. My imagination goes into overdrive.'

'Sorry. I hate that too, but really, it doesn't matter.'

Nesta's expression grew concerned. 'It's about William, isn't it? You've seen him with another girl? You know something about him that you don't want me to know . . .'

'Nooooooooo. No. Course not. It's not about William. OK. It's . . . it's about Luke.'

'Luke?'

'Yes. I saw him when I was out jogging and we went for a coffee and . . .'

'You're still crazy about him?'

I nodded.

'How does he feel?'

'Sorry. Said he was sorry. But pleased to see me and . . . look, I'm sorry too, Nesta, but I still really like him a lot. And I think he'd like to see me again but I'd never ever, ever do it if it made you unhappy for an instant, because our friendship is a million times more important than he is.'

'Only a million, huh?'

'Squillion.'

Nesta was thoughtful for a moment, then she nodded to herself as if she'd made up her mind about something. 'Go for it,' she said. 'I mean it. Go for it. He was always yours. I always kind of knew that, and if he'd met you before me then there wouldn't have been the mix up. Besides, I have William now. It would be mean of me to pull a strop for no good reason.'

'You sure?'

She made a sign of the cross over me. 'Go in peace. You have my blessing.'

I laughed. 'Sure? Double sure?'

'Triple,' she said, as she linked arms with me and we walked into school. 'Hey, but what about the gorgeous Ollie Axford? Shame to see him go to waste.'

I grimaced. 'Well, see here's the thing: I like Ollie too, and at this stage, to be honest, I'm still not exactly sure about Luke. I just wanted to check out how you felt first, because if you didn't want me to see him again, then I wouldn't. Not for a second. So that was number one on the to-do list. Next is to check out the Luke situation. Is he involved at the mo, because if he is, then no way am I getting caught up with him.'

Nesta laughed. 'Wow, you sound organised!'

'Just . . . I don't want to get hurt again, you know . . . after last time . . .'

Nesta nodded. 'Course. And I don't blame you. But I can check the Luke situation. Don't forget, William knows him.'

'Oh. OK. If you don't mind, but, er . . . Nesta, will you do it . . . you know . . . subtly?'

Nesta looked horrified that I could ask such a thing, but she has got a big mouth sometimes.

'How else?' she said.

'Well, I wouldn't want it to get back to Luke that I'd been asking about him or anything, especially as nothing may happen.'

Nesta tapped the side of her nose. 'Trust me.'

'And I'm going to check out Ollie. For all I know, he may have a whole harem of girls. If he's available and really is interested in me then I'll decide between them.'

'Cool,' said Nesta. 'Sounds like a plan. And I'm sure it will become clear who is the real contender.'

'You think?'

'Yeah. Like if it's meant to be, it's meant to be. As our Iz always says, fate or destiny will make it clear.'

Later that day, another man came back into my life.

When I got back from school, Mum was arguing with him in the hallway.

'Go to your bed this instant!' she commanded.

Dad rolled his eyes to the ceiling then beckoned me over to him. 'Oh, for heaven's sake, give me a break,' he said to Mum as we hugged each other. 'I'm fine. I'm going to work on the computer and that's not strenuous, it's just sitting. Hello, daughter.'

'Hi, Dad,' I said. It felt great to see him back on familiar ground again, harrumphing around like he normally did. 'I got Mum's message that you'd be back this afternoon so I got some DVDs on the way home for you. You could lie on the sofa and watch them.'

'I could,' said Dad. 'I *could*, but I have some calls to make. Better things to do than lie about watching DVDs!'

'Everything's taken care of both here and at work,' said Mum. 'You can relax. I've taken a week's leave to look after you and Dr Miller said you *have* to take it easy. You know you should.'

'I will. All in good time,' said Dad. 'But first there are things to do. There's a pile of mail for one thing, plus I'm expecting Dr Rollands. He wanted to pop in to see me at the hospital again, so I told him that they were letting me out and to come here.'

Mum sighed but I started to laugh. Whether at home or at the hospital, Dad proved to be a difficult patient who wouldn't do as he was told.

'And TJ,' he said when he spotted me laughing. 'Go and make me a cheese sandwich, will you? With tomatoes. And plenty of mayonnaise. It's been hours since I had that lunch you sent me, which was delicious by the way.'

'Cheese? Mayo? Richard,' said Mum, 'we have to look at your diet. All that fat is not good for someone with your condition.'

Dad rolled his eyes.

'Lucy's dad runs the health shop in Muswell Hill,' I said. 'He says you are what you eat and I've heard him says loads of times that people can change their health by changing their diet. I've seen loads of tip sheets in there to help various conditions. Would you like me to pick one up for you?'

'I would not. I know all about that stuff. I'd rather have a cheese sandwich and die happy than eat brown rice and lentils and be miserable,' said Dad. 'Oh, come on. I'm just out of hospital. I've been dreaming of a decent sandwich. And excuse me, but *who* is the doctor round here? I know what's good for me and what's not.'

This time, both Mum and I sighed. You couldn't tell Dad anything as he always thought he knew best even though Mum was a doctor too.

At that moment, the doorbell rang.

I opened it to find that it was Dad's friend, Dr Rollands.

'What are you doing out of bed, man?' he said when he saw Dad in the hallway.

Dad threw up his hands in exasperation. 'Can a man get no peace in his own home?' he exclaimed, then stomped into the living room.

Dr Rollands then proceeded to have a discussion with Mum about Dad and his condition, his progress and so on.

It was funny because, unseen by them, I could see Dad was listening from behind the door.

' . . . Hmmm, yes, I can see that,' said Dr Rollands. 'Must be difficult. But then he always was stubborn. What he needs is to get away. Somewhere quiet with no distractions. Complete rest and recuperation.'

'OHHH for heaven's sake,' said Dad coming out from his hiding place. 'I'm fine. Get away? Are you mad? Travel is one of the most stressful things on the planet. Delays. Traffic. All the yobs you have to mix with to get where you going. Strange beds to sleep in. No, forget it. I'm staying here. And if no one is going to make me that cheese sandwich, I'll do it myself!'

Dr Rollands put his hand on Dad's back and ushered him into the living room where he made him sit down. He then produced an envelope from his briefcase. 'Ah, now that's where you're wrong,' he said as he pulled a number of photos out of the envelope. 'Take a look at these.'

I went over to Dad's chair and looked over his shoulder. Inside the envelope there were photographs of an idyllic detached pink cottage in a garden full of flowers.

'Cornwall,' said Dr Rollands. 'You couldn't find a more peaceful spot if you tried.'

'Yes. Lovely. So?' Dad asked.

'So. It's mine and I'm offering it to you and your family,' said Dr Rollands. 'It's been our second home for years and we were down there every summer while the boys were growing up, but now they've flown the coup. We won't be using it this year; in fact, we seem to be spending more and more time in France. The place is yours if you want it as a place to go and recuperate for a week or so.'

Mum took the photos and had a look. 'We do love that part of the world, don't we, Richard? And Marie will be close by in Devon. In fact, we even thought of moving down there last year, didn't we?'

'But you're not going to?' I asked, as a sudden panic hit me. 'You knocked that idea on the head, right?'

Dad nodded. 'Don't worry, TJ. No. We decided we'd miss London too much, but . . .' he took the photos and had another look. 'It does seem tempting. What's it like inside? Water? Heating? All mod cons? I can't be doing with any of these go-back-to-nature-type trips away.'

'Do me a favour,' said Dr Rollands. 'There's a computer there with Internet. The cottage even has cable. All the sports channels. And the movies.'

After Dr Rollands had left, while I made Dad his sandwich, Mum and Dad had a chat. For once they seemed to be in agreement.

Mum got on the phone fast to make arrangements. She didn't want to waste any time. The plan was that she and Dad would drive down there on Sunday so that Dad could begin his recuperation as soon as possible. My brother Paul would come up to stay with me in the interim and then we'd drive down to join them a week later for half-term. And she also called Lucy's dad to ask him to pop in with the diet sheet.

'He may be a top surgeon,' she said to me after she'd put the phone down, 'but nutrition is not always top of the agenda with any of them. It's never too late to learn some good new habits.'

'Could be fab,' said Izzie, when I told her the plan later on the phone. 'But you'll be away for a week leaving me alone with the love-bubble couples. Lucy and Tony. Nesta and William. And Izzie and Izzie. I'll be a billy loner. What am I going to do without you?'

'We can text, and apparently there's a computer there so we can e-mail.'

'In that case,' said Izzie, 'I'm going to do something that I've been meaning to do for ages: set up a private chat room for the four of us so we can all talk while you're away without it costing a fortune.'

'Excellent idea,' I said.

'I'll do it next week so it's ready for half-term. So . . . a week up here with Luke with no parents to cramp your style? Hmmm. Could be interesting.'

'Maybe it's meant to be, hey?' I said, hopefully.

'Ah, but with whom? It's worked out perfectly for you to spend the half-term down in Cornwall with your other lover.'

'What other lover? I don't know anyone down there . . .'

'Er, come on, stupid. Get your brain in gear. Where do the Axfords live?'

'Oh my God! Yes. Cornwall. I'd forgotten that the Axfords have a house down there. Because Ollie is at school in

Kensington, I think of him as a Londoner. But it's bound to be miles away from where we'll be. Cornwall is an enormous place.'

'Hold on, I've got the copy of *Vogue* with the article on Star Axford in it – Lucy left it here last week,' said Izzie. 'I think it even mentioned where the house was.'

The phone went quiet for a while.

'Iz. *Iz,* are you still there?'

A moment later, she came back on the phone. 'Rame Peninsula,' she said. 'Where's the house you'll be staying?'

'Not sure. Just a mo.'

I ran out into the hall and called down the stairs. 'Hey, Mum. Where in Cornwall is Dr Rolland's house?'

'The Rame Peninsula, dear,' she called back.

'Ohmigod!' I said, as I went back to the phone.

'I know,' said Izzie. 'I heard. It's destiny.'

E-mail: **Outbox (1)**
To: hannahnutter@fastmail.com
From: babewithbrains@psnet.co.uk
Date: 21st May
Subject: God

Hey Hannahlulu,

Sorree it's bin so long.

A million things have been happening this end.

Dad was ill but he's better now, thank God. Talking of which or who, have you any idea if there is one? A God, that is. And if there is, have you got his address as no one over here seems to have it and it's not in the Yellow Pages cos I've looked. A phone number, website or e-mail address would do. An official www.god.com would be a gas, wouldn't it? We could just go to a site and leave a message for him? As in, Dear God, heeeeelp. Why am I here? Where have I come from? What happens after you die? Why did you create wasps?

Lucy says there has to be a God cos of all the beautiful things in nature.

Nesta says we all have pea brains and it's too big a question for us to grasp the answer, so we should just get on and enjoy life.

Izzie's still looking.

And I don't know.

U wouldn't believe what else is happening. Not one boy but two in the running. Ollie Axford. His dad is a famous rock and roller. Ollie is mucho cute. And the other boy is Luke. Remember him? Cause of big trouble last Christmas. I thought he was my soulmate. Still do, maybe. Don't know what's going to happen though as it's early days . . . watch this space.

Stay in touch.

Luv and stuff
TJ.

## Chapter 8

# Liberation

'Byeee. Have a great time.' I called as Mum waved from the driving seat.

Dad waved from the back of the car, where he was sitting like royalty, propped up with pillows and blankets.

Mum started the engine and off they went.

When the car disappeared round the corner of our road, Paul and I turned and went into the house. It felt so quiet after the flurry of activity in the last few days. Mum had done endless shopping trips so that cupboards and the freezer were stuffed with quick and easy meals. Mr Lovering had been over with boxes of health foods. Dad had patiently sat and listened to what he had to say about 'you are what you eat,' then pulled faces at the bags of oats and lentils when he'd gone. For a wrinkly, Dad could act really childishly sometimes, but I think he liked Mr Lovering as I heard them laughing about something. Probably the time he caught Lucy bouncing on my bed wearing a bra on her head. And then of course there was the packing. And repacking. Mum was unsure what to take as, with it being only May, the weather could turn colder again. In the end, she packed things for all seasons, and it had been good to see her back to her normal self, smiling and singing as she went about the house organising everything and everyone.

'So just us, kid,' said Paul as I closed the front door.

'Yep,' I said. 'Quiet, isn't it?'

'Yep,' said Paul. He went into the sitting room, scanned the CDs then put one in and turned the volume up.

Rock music blasted out so loud that it made the room vibrate. We both began to play air guitar and throw our heads around like mad heavy metal stars. A look that Paul had down well as with his long hair and denims, he does look like a scruffy musician.

Two seconds later, there was a loud knock on the window. We both looked up to see Mum's angry face.

'Oops,' said Paul and motioned for me to turn the music down.

As the house grew silent again, we both raced into the hall and Paul opened the door.

'What on *earth* is going on?' demanded Mum. 'I've been gone less than five minutes and you're acting like teenagers.'

I didn't think that now was the time to say, 'Er, actually I *am* a teenager'.

Paul shifted about on his feet like a naughty ten-year-old. 'Sorry . . . Just . . .'

'I don't know,' said Mum. 'Maybe this wasn't such a good idea, I mean you're barely out of your teens yourself, Paul. Can I trust you?'

'We were just being silly,' he said. 'And I'd say that twenty-three is well out of my teens, not barely. We'll be fine. Don't worry. I'll make sure she's in bed by ten every night and let her take mind-expanding drugs only on Fridays. I'll only allow boys up into her room on the weekend and absolutely no vodka unless she's got friends round.'

Mum slapped his arm lightly. 'Good job I know you're joking,' she said, 'although that's not funny at all.'

'So why've you come back?' Paul asked.

Mum spotted a bag in the hall. 'Forgot our supplies for the journey. Now, TJ, I know you're a sensible girl so I expect you to behave. And Paul, I want you to take this responsibility seriously. No staying out late on school nights. Early to bed . . .'

'Mum, we've been through all this,' said Paul and ushered her back to the door. 'Go. Enjoy. We'll both be fine.'

We stood at the door and waved them off for a second time.

As soon as we saw the car disappear around the corner of our road again, Paul dashed back into the sitting room, turned the CD back on full blast and came back into the hall where we both giggled at each other and resumed our air guitar playing.

Paul can be a real laugh, although Mum and Dad don't exactly appreciate that side of him at the moment. They had such high hopes for him when he got top As in his A-levels. They thought that he'd follow in the family footsteps and go to medical school. He did for a year, but wasn't happy so he dropped out and went travelling to India, Morocco and Ethiopia. He's been back in England for a few months now and still isn't sure what he wants to do. For the time being he's freelancing as a painter and decorator in Bristol, and Mum and Dad (especially Dad) aren't happy about it at all. They want him to get a 'proper' job. Paul insists that being a decorator is as proper as it gets, but he knows what they mean. He told me that he still doesn't have a clue what he wants to do so, until then, he's painting to earn a bit of dosh and pass the time.

Luckily Mum didn't come back a second time, and after our spate of guitar playing I went up to get ready for football practice. While I was changing, Ollie Axford called.

'Got a spare ticket for the Cirque Du Soleil,' he said. 'Ever seen them?'

'No. Are they like a proper circus?'

'Better,' he said. 'They're amazing. Beautiful. Hard to describe. You've got to see them. It's like an alien race has landed and come to entertain us.'

'When?'

'Thursday night. Albert Hall. Star was supposed to come with me, but she's had a last-minute booking for a job in Milan. So you up for it? Might mean a bit of a late night. I know your Goody Two Shoes sub-personality won't be able to come as it's a school night, but maybe one of the others could. Tell your mum I'll put her in a cab.'

I felt flattered that Ollie had not only remembered about my sub-personalities but also their names. 'Hold on, I'll ask,' I said and raced down to ask Paul.

'No problem,' he said. 'Cirque Du Soleil are brill. You have to see them.'

Great, I thought, as I went back to the phone. Life without the wrinklies was going to be fun.

The next few days were brilliant. Liberating. Paul let me stay up late. We ate what we wanted when we wanted. Coco Pops for supper and cold pizza for breakfast. We played more loud music. And, best of all, Izzie, Nesta and Lucy came over to my house on Sunday afternoon after Mum and Dad had left and then every night after school. Partly to just hang out in a parent-free zone and partly to get stuck into painting my bedroom. I hadn't even given the decorating a thought while Dad was in hospital and would have put it on hold even longer if he hadn't insisted that I go ahead with it and no arguing! I said I would be happy to take the paint back to Homebase and have the room white, but he wouldn't hear of it. He said that I had to take advantage of Paul's skills before he went back to Bristol and that I decorate in the colours that I wanted, no expense spared.

Paul was 'site manager' and did the ceiling and most of the difficult work while I was out at school, but us girls did some of the woodwork. By the time Tuesday evening came, most of it had been done and the room looked transformed from a drab interior to a fresh but cosy room.

'Tomorrow evening after school we'll do Camden,' said Lucy as she surveyed our work. 'Look for nick-nacks.'

'And then we'll have some time for beautification,' said Izzie. 'Please. My skin and nails need some attention.'

'And I need to start getting ready for my date with Ollie,' I said.

Nesta laughed. 'I thought I was bad. Your date is on Thursday. Are you saying you need a whole twenty-four hours to get ready?'

'Yep,' I said. 'I need all the time and help I can get.'

'What about Luke?' asked Izzie. 'Is he out of the picture now?'

I looked at Nesta, who tapped her nose. 'I just have to do a little detective work on Monsieur Luke. Sorry, TJ, I haven't had a chance to get William on his own and I don't want to ask him on the phone in case Luke is sitting right there with him. I should see him on Thursday and will deliver my report as soon as poss on Friday morning.'

'And I'll date the divine Ollie Axford for an evening,' I said, 'and deliver my report back and then you can all help me decide.'

'Sounds good to me,' said Lucy. 'Although it's your decision in the end.'

'I know,' I said. After what happened last time with Luke with everything feeling so secret and underhand, this time I wanted to let everyone know what was happening at all stages so that there could be no weird feelings. 'And hey, let's have the beauty session here. We can play music and run around with our face packs on without worrying that Tony or your brothers are going to see us.'

'Cool,' said Izzie. 'Though what about Paul?'

'Oh, he'll want to join in, probably,' I replied. 'He's always nicking my moisturiser.'

And so it was settled. It felt good to be able to have my friends over without worrying about upsetting Dad or making too much noise. Life was just getting better and better and there was still the date with Ollie to come.


The week seemed to fly by and, before I knew it, it was Thursday evening. I got the Tube down to Kensington High Street then walked along to the Albert Hall. I wasn't sure how long it would take so I'd set off in plenty of time. The last thing I wanted was to be late. I ended up being half an hour early and, not wanting to seem too keen, I went over to the park opposite and sat on a bench to pass the time. It was a warm evening for May and it seemed like half of London was in the park enjoying the weather and the other half were swarming about the Albert Hall, ready to go in and watch Cirque Du Soleil.

I said I'd meet Ollie at seven-fifteen, so at ten past seven, I got up, crossed the road and looked for him amongst the crowd of people outside and flowing into the reception area. He was standing on the steps by the entry and waved when he saw me.

'Hey,' he said as he kissed my cheek and handed me a carton of juice. 'There you are. You look great. I got here early so went and got us something to drink.'

'Yunuh . . .' I started, then laughed as I knew that he knew that I was talking alien-speak.

'Cool,' he said. 'That's Noola, isn't it? She's the one who comes through when you fancy someone?'

'Uh . . .' I nodded, then felt myself blush furiously. What was the matter with me this evening? I'd managed to be totally normal with him last time we'd met, but seeing him again was having a strange effect on me. He seemed to get better-looking each time I saw him, even though by the look of his black jacket and loosened black and yellow striped tie, he was still in his school uniform.

'Sorry I didn't have time to change,' he said as if reading my thoughts. 'Had a drama rehearsal that went on a bit late.'

'It's OK. Your uniform suits you. So what play are you doing?'

'*Romeo and Juliet.* I've got the lead so I couldn't miss the rehearsal. I had to fly to get here. Didn't think I was going to make it but I ended up being early. I often do that – I hate being late for people.'

'Me too,' I said. 'So the lead, huh? Juliet? I bet you look gorgeous as a girl. Who's playing Romeo?'

'Oh, ha ha. *I'm* Romeo . . .'

'I knew that,' I said. 'Just joshing.'

As he took my hand and led me through the mass of people arriving and eager to get inside, Luke flashed into my mind. Funny how both he and Ollie were interested in acting.

'Shall we go and find our seats?' asked Ollie.

The effect of his hand in mine made my brain go blank. 'Yuhnuh. I mean *yes* . . .' I blustered, as inwardly I told myself to chill.

Inside the air was buzzing with anticipation as people took their seats, chatted, stood up for late-comers, got out glasses, turned off mobile phones and generally settled themselves for the show.

'This place is stunning,' I said as we took our seats in the vast red and gold circular hall.

'How's your dad?' whispered Ollie as the lights dimmed.

'Really good,' I whispered back. 'He and Mum have gone down to a country cottage to recuperate. Actually, it might be near you. It's on the Rame Peninsula.'

'You're kidding! Where? What's the address?'

'Um. Rose Harbour Cottage, I think. It's in a private bay . . .'

'I know it,' said Ollie. 'Pink?"

'Yeah.'

'It's near where I go walking when I'm down there. So . . . this is all a bit fast, isn't it? So who's looking after you?'

'Paul,' I said. 'My brother. We've been having a real laugh.'

I wasn't sure whether it was the lighting in the hall or my imagination, but Ollie's eyes seem to glint with interest. 'Oh, really?'

I nodded. 'Paul's driving us down this Saturday to join Mum and Dad.'

Ollie grinned. 'This is sooo cool. And I'm going on Sunday. Fantastic. I can show you around.'

He tucked his hand through my arm, slipped his hand into mine and squeezed it. Our second date. And now the promise of half-term. Did this mean we were becoming an item? I wondered. Item as in boyfriend/girlfriend? For a moment I felt panic as I wasn't sure if I was ready. I still had Luke to check out before I committed myself to one boy. Oh God, oh God, I thought, I am worse than most boys. I have commitment phobia.

I didn't have a chance to give it much more thought as soon I got totally caught up in the show. It was breathtaking. A mix of dance, opera, rock music and acrobatics, with the most fabulous costumes and stunning light effects. It was like being transported to a dream world, as Ollie had said, of beautiful aliens who could do things with their bodies that made my eyes water just to look at them. We watched tightrope dancers, clowns, trapeze artists, jugglers, stiltwalkers, contortionists – probably about forty of them in all – who performed to the accompaniment of musicians. Each performer seemed to have taken their particular art and perfected it. I watched spellbound and, for a while, even forgot that I was sitting next to Ollie.

When we got outside after the show, Ollie made his way on to the pavement. He seemed to be looking for someone.

'I prebooked a car,' he said. 'Seemed the best option as we'd never get a cab here at this time of night.'

I had to admit that it seemed like he'd made the right decision as already I could see a queue of people waiting for taxis and only one in sight. Paul had acted the worried parent when I left and made sure I had twenty-five pounds for my taxi fare home. It was really sweet of him as I know he'd given it to me out of his own money and he didn't have much at the moment.

'Ah, there he is,' said Ollie as he spotted a driver, complete with chauffeur's cap, leaning against the bonnet of a white limo a short distance away. 'Come on.'

He waved at the chauffeur, took my arm and ushered me towards the car that was waiting about a hundred yards up the road.

'But . . .' I started. I only had the money that Paul had given me in my purse. No way could I afford to pay the fare for a car like the one waiting for us. 'It's OK, Ollie. I'll get the Tube.'

'On your own at this time of night? No way.'

'I can call my brother to meet me at the station.'

Ollie shook his head. 'It's my duty to see you home and I will.'

'I . . . I . . . Ollie, I can't afford a car like that.'

Ollie stopped, turned and looked at me. 'What kind of cheapskate boys have you been going out with, TJ? Like, no way would I ask you to pay. I'm paying. Actually no, my dad's paying. He has an account with the company. Mum and Dad always use these cars while they're in London and he lets me use one whenever I need. Dad likes these cars because they allow him to be private – they have those tinted windows where the passengers can see out but no one can see in.'

'If you're sure . . .'

'No biggie, come on,' he said and waved. 'Hey, Peter.'

The chauffeur waved back. 'Mr Axford,' he said, and opened the door to the back seat. Ollie turned, grinned and raised an eyebrow at me as if he found it all amusing.

A moment later I was sitting on plush leather seats being chauffeured through the streets of London. I felt like a princess.

'Do you want to go and eat somewhere?' asked Ollie. 'My treat?'

'Oh. No thanks. That is, thanks for asking but I ate before I came out and . . .'

Ollie smiled and patted my knee. 'School night and SP Goody Two Shoes is out?'

'Maybe. A bit,' I replied feeling like a twelve-year-old. Get a grip, I told myself. I so wished I had a grown-up sophisticated type of alter ego because I could certainly use her at the moment. Maybe I'd act the part anyway. That's what Nesta told me she does when she feels out of her depth. She picks a character from a movie and pretends that she's her. I'd pretend that I was Lady Penelope out of Thunderbirds.

'Drink?' asked Ollie, as he opened a mini-bar in front of us.

I nodded and put on a posh voice. 'Yar, please. Champagne. Vintage. Oh, and I'll have some caviar while you're at it, my man.'

Ollie pulled a half bottle of champagne out and held it up. 'Think this is vintage, not sure we have any caviar though.'

'Oh! I was only joking . . .'

'You can have some if you want. I'm going to,' said Ollie, popping the cork. He leant forward again and found two glasses, poured the champagne and handed one to me.

'Oh. Thanks,' I said, as I took the glass and debated whether to have some or not. Stop being such a baby, I told myself. I'd never had champagne before and, as I sipped it, I felt little bubbles go up the back of my nose. It was nice, like pop. I decided not to tell Ollie that I hadn't had champagne before as I didn't want him to think that I was immature.

Ollie leaned forward again, flicked a switch and some sultry music began to play through speakers behind us.

'Hmmm, cool music,' I said.

'Yeah. Dad always requests it so they always have the CD when there's an Axford booking.'

'Yeah. It's good.'

'To us,' said Ollie, and clinked his glass with mine.

'To us,' I replied, thinking I knew exactly which of Ollie's sub-personalities was present at the moment. Casanova. He was *sooo* smooth.

I sat back and looked out of the window as the car glided through the dark streets of the city. It felt so sophisticated and I couldn't wait to tell Lucy, Izzie and Nesta about it in the morning.

As the car cruised up towards North London, I began to wonder why we hadn't stopped off at Ollie's school.

'Didn't you say your school was in Kensington?' I asked. 'That's just down the road from the Albert Hall. I thought we'd be dropping you off.'

He nodded. 'Just seeing you home safely first.'

'Oh, you don't need to do that,' I said. 'I'll be fine.'

Ollie stuck his bottom lip out. 'Don't you want me here?'

'Oh. No. *No*. It's not that. I didn't want to put you out.'

Ollie leaned over and brushed my lips with his, sending a tingly sensation up and down my spine. 'You're not putting me out,' he said, then he put down his glass and moved in closer.

We spent the rest of the journey snogging our faces off and I don't know whether it was the champagne, the soulful music, the buzz of riding in the back of a limo or Ollie, but it felt faaaanbubblytastic.

Before I knew it, we were cruising down our road. I hoped that some of the neighbours were up so that they could see the car and watch me getting out of it. I could just imagine their tongues wagging the next day. Thank God Mum and Dad were away as they would have had a fit.

'What number is it again?' asked Ollie.

'Number eseven.'

'Seven?' asked Ollie.

'Elesen,' I said.

Ollie laughed. 'I think you're a bit piddled, TJ Watts,' he said.

'Nah,' I said. 'I don't drink. Elesen. Eleven.'

Ollie laughed again. 'I think I'd better see you in.'

That woke me up. 'Oh. No! Be OK.'

The house was in a mess as, although Paul and I had meant to clear up, we'd kept putting it off. There were takeaway cartons in the kitchen and we hadn't done the washing-up since last night. And I hadn't moved back into my room yet after the decorating so all my stuff was all over the upstairs hall. No. Ollie coming in was not an option. I snuggled into him to distract him from the idea. 'One more song?'

Ollie leaned forward, opened the partition to the front and said something to the driver. Then he closed the partition, turned the music up and leaned back with me again.

Once again, we started kissing. It was nice. Very nice. Snuggly, cosy. Everything seemed to be merging together, the music, the smell of leather, the sensation of Ollie's lips on mine. I could really get to like this lifestyle, I thought, as I ran my fingers through Ollie's hair.

Ollie sighed and pulled me closer and then . . . was it my imagination or was his hand creeping up my inner thigh? No. It was on my knee. That's OK. No. No. It was definitely creeping up. Ohmigod, I thought. This is it. What do I do? This is what Lucy's been on about with Tony. Wandering hands. Or maybe not. No. Ollie's hand left my leg and came up to my waist. More kissing. Phew. He must have changed his mind about trying anything. Must remember to soak the paint brushes in turps before we leave for Cornwall. (Cripes! Where did that come from?) Oh no, Ollie had gone back to my knee and, oh no, his hand was moving up again. It was so weird because it partly made me feel tingly and partly made me go rigid with panic, like, what was he going to do next and how should I react? Whatever, I knew that I didn't want him to do any more than he was already doing. I put my hand over his and moved it up to my waist. Big mistake. It gave him *totally* the wrong idea. He cupped my right breast in his hand, gently squeezed and let out a groan.

'Oh, TJ . . .'

Oh jumping Jonahs, I thought, as I moved his hand down again. Back up it went. My head began to clear fast. I am so not ready for this, I thought. It's only our second date. He'll think I'm so easy if I let him carry on. And yet if I stop him, will he think I'm a baby? But he did pay for the tickets for the circus and organise the car home. But no. No. This doesn't feel right. I don't owe him anything just because he paid for everything. No. I don't want to do this.

I pushed him away.

'Wha . . .?'

'Stop it,' I said, and slid over to get out of the car.

'But I thought you wanted to . . .'

'Well, you thought wrong.'

I opened the car door and leaned down to pick up my bag.

'TJ. TJ. Don't go. I'm sorry. I thought you wanted to.'

I got out, slammed the car door shut and ran into the house.

I felt so confused. Had I given off signals that I'd wanted to go further? If I had, they weren't intentional. Had I led him on or was he just trying it on? I fumbled with my key at the door. I desperately wanted to get inside. I wasn't ready to be sophisticated. I wasn't ready to deal with boys' fumblings and being grown up. I didn't know how to be.

All I wanted was Mojo and to get under my duvet and hide.

E-mail: **Inbox (1)**
To: babewithbrains@psnet.co.uk
From: hannahnutter@fastmail.com
Date: 25th May
Subject: Oh my God!

Darlingus TJ
Gordie Lobachops! How vunderba to hear from you.

And karambo!!! Ollie Axford as in Zac Axford's son. F . . . f . . . fab fabarooney. I looked him up on the Internet. He's like mega!!! Dad Axford, that is. There were loads of sites about him and a pic of the family. So glam. Two sisters and Ollie wollie dingle dangle doodle all the way. He looks sooooo cute. Don't be a picky poo person, make sure you pick the right one.

Let me know how it goes and all and all cor blimey love a duck! You can text me as well as e-mail, yuno.

Life over here in sunshine land is happy dappy. Love life okee dokee, new boy from down under at school. We call him Bruce but his name is Dan. Cute as pie and I have offered to show him around. Hahahahahaha.

Miss my mates over there in Englandy land.

Toodleoo.
Hannahharmonicus

PS: Give luvie dovie smackeroo kisses to Scary Dad and tell him that he's still my pin-up! Glad he's OK.
PPS: Will get back to you on the God front! I'll see if anyone over here knows anything . . . You never know.

# Chapter 9

# Luke

'Has he called since?' asked Nesta after I'd filled them in on the latest in the break at school on Friday morning.

'Twice,' I said. 'And left a text saying sorry, sorry. I haven't answered his calls or the text. I don't know what to say. See, it wasn't just the groping. It was how it made me feel. Really mixed up. Like a hundred thoughts were going through my mind all at the same time and I thought, God, I hope it's not like this the first time I have sex. You know, that I'm focusing on the experience but also wondering if I've given in too soon, wondering if he thinks I'm a kid, am I any good at it, not to mention thinking about paintbrushes.'

'Paintbrushes?' asked Lucy.

'Yeah. Out of the blue, mid-kiss, I suddenly remembered I hadn't put the paintbrushes in to soak. I mean, how unromantic is that?'

At that moment Miss Watkins came out of the classroom and saw us propped up against the wall in the corridor. 'Outside, you girls. It's a lovely day. Go and get some fresh air.'

'I've had that,' said Izzie as we all pushed ourselves up and headed for the playground. 'Like you're kissing someone and part of your mind is thinking that you need to make a phone call or something.'

'I think you only get that when it's boring,' said Nesta. 'If it's the right person then all that matters is the sensation of being with them . . .'

'Oh, I don't know,' said Lucy. 'It can depend on the mood that you're in. Like with Tony and I, sometimes it's magic and other times, I think about other stuff. I think it gets like that when you've been with someone a while. The passion fades and paintbrushes or phone calls or whatever can take over sometimes.'

'Well, all I know is that what had started out as a great evening went flat,' I said.

Izzie linked arms with me as we reached the playground and headed for our favourite bench in the far corner. 'Hey,' she said. 'Don't worry. Most boys have octopus arms and hands. Lucy gets it all the time, don't you?''

'Yeah. But that's just it,' I said. 'She's been going with Tony for *ages*. Over a year on and off . . .'

'And on and off and on and off,' said Izzie, laughing.

'And he's been behaving lately,' said Lucy.

'But this was only my *second* date with Ollie. *First* date if you don't count meeting in the bookshop. I mean, who does he think I am? Do you think I have a sign on my head that says, *Hello boys, I'm easy*?'

Nesta grinned and looked at my chest. 'Er . . . Not on your head, dearie.'

Lucy linked my other arm. 'Maybe it *was* that top that I made you for the Diamond Destiny dance. He can't stop thinking about your jelubis . . .' She put her hands over her boobs and made a jiggling motion and we all cracked up.

'Yes,' said Izzie. 'He'll be sending you postcards for the rest of your life. From Peru, from India, from Scunthorpe. Oh TJ. T . . . T T T . . . J. I just caaaan't stop thinking about your magnificent jelubis.'

'You looked very nice in that outfit,' said Nesta. 'Don't let some stupid boy who's got the hots stop you dressing like a hottie . . .'

'Well, some boys might say I was asking for it,' I said.

'Well, they need a sock in the face,' said Nesta. 'It gets me so mad that sometimes a girl can't wear something pretty without some twerp thinking that the only reason she's doing it is because she wants some oik to ogle her or grope her. As if. Listen, TJ, don't worry and don't start dressing down again. You, *we* in fact, need to learn how to handle these sorts of situations and if it doesn't feel right, then learn to say, Oi you, noooo. And without feeling bad about it or guilty or obligated or worried that they might think you're a lesbian. Ollie was trying his luck, that's all. It's not your fault. Cute though he is, I had him figured for a player from the start.'

'But I think he does genuinely like you,' said Izzie. 'You said no to him but he's called since and apologised. That has to mean something.'

'Yeah,' said Lucy. 'He must like you.'

'Did you ask him about other girls?' asked Izzie.

'No. I meant to. We didn't get round to it.'

'Too busy playing backseat wrestling,' said Nesta. 'But talking of other girls, I have done my homework *à la* Luke situation and, according to William, Luke hasn't been out with anyone since before Christmas.'

'Christmas?' said Lucy. 'Veeeery interesting. Isn't that when you both broke up with him?'

'Yep. I think he's still interested in you, TJ,' she said. 'So does William.'

'Er . . . Actually he called a couple of times last night and left a message when I was out. Asked if I'd meet him for an hour this evening in the café at Jackson's Lane. Said he has something to say.'

'Are you going to go?' asked Lucy.

I nodded. 'I already called and left a message. I got his voicemail but I said I would.'

Izzie rolled her eyes. 'Some girls have all the luck. Not one buff boy after you but two. Hey, give us one if one's going spare.'

'Oh, but you can have either one if you want. You know . . .'

Izzie punched my arm. 'I don't fancy either of them. You know that. Not that I don't appreciate that they are both cute, just they're not my type. I'm not worried, though. I looked up the progressions in my horoscope last night and it said that I'd have to wait until later in the summer before love comes my way.'

'What are progressions?' asked Lucy.

'The progress of your birth chart,' Izzie replied. 'Like what's coming up next.'

'Did you look up ours?' asked Nesta.

Izzie nodded. 'Lucy's is steady at the moment. Which we all know. Things with Tony going nicely.'

'We agreed no complications while he does his A-levels, and they're coming up next month,' said Lucy. 'He's studying like mad. No two-timing. No wandering hands on his side and no dumping him on my side. He needs to focus. And then . . . we'll see. If he gets into Oxford, and I'm sure he will, I have to let go.'

Izzie was looking at Lucy with a soft expression when she said this. A cross between sadness and concern, and I thought, hmmmm, Izzie has read something else in Lucy's horoscope that she's not saying. I hope it's not going to be painful when Tony goes but then goodbyes are always hard.

'What about mine?' asked Nesta.

Izzie's face brightened. 'Fun, fun, fun. No worries there, Nesta. Venus is brilliantly aspected in your chart at the moment.'

'And, er . . . mine?' I asked.

'Ah . . .' said Izzie. 'Yes. Um . . . interesting times ahead for you, TJ. Venus is square to Saturn, which means some major life lessons are to be learned about love and stuff.'

'Major life lessons? Woopeedoop,' I said unenthusiastically. 'Sounds like fun. Not.'

I arrived to meet Luke at Jackson's Lane fifteen minutes late. Everything had conspired against me. After realising that I'd drunk alcohol when I was out with Ollie, Paul had had a personality change and given me the third degree about where I was going and who with and what time I'd be back. Honestly, not even a full week and he'd turned into Scary Dad. I finally got away after he demanded that I keep my mobile on and that I was back at a reasonable hour. I tried pleading with him that it was Friday and now half-term, so no school in the morning, but he kept on about how we had to close up the house tomorrow and pack and be on the road for Cornwall by midday. I don't think he likes responsibility very much.

And then there was a delay on the Tube. Signal failure at Whetstone, so I ended up half walking, half jogging. I hadn't wanted to do that as the weather had turned cloudy and was threatening rain – there was one thing damp weather did to my hair and that was turn it frizzy . . . and I wanted to look good when I saw Luke.

Unfortunately he was already there when I arrived, so I didn't even get the chance to go to the Ladies and reapply my lip-gloss or comb out the tangles in my hair.

'Hi,' I said as I sat down opposite him at the table he had taken in the café area. 'Sorry I'm late. I . . .'

'Hey,' he said and leaned over and took one of my hands in both of his. 'You look gorgeous. I'm *so* glad you came. I was beginning to wonder if you were going to show.'

'I said I would. So. You said you had something to say?'

Luke sat back with a serious expression on his face. 'Wow. Right. Yeah. Straight to the point. OK. Yes. I do have something to say.' He leaned forward, took my hands again and looked deeply into my eyes. I felt my chest tighten as a familiar feeling hit the pit of my stomach. There was no denying it. There was some very powerful chemistry between Luke and me. 'OK. I'm just going to come out with it, TJ. I know I blew it last time . . . with you and Nesta and not telling Nesta that it was over when I should have. I've been cursing myself ever since. I know we have something special. You feel it, don't you?'

'I . . .' I did feel it, but I wasn't sure if I wanted to expose myself so readily. I'd got so hurt last time. 'I know that there's something but, well, it was awful. I almost lost Nesta as a mate and I really value her. All those girls in fact.'

'I know and I'm really sorry . . .'

Suddenly all the feelings for him that I'd made myself bury threatened to come to the surface. I mustn't let them, I thought as I took a deep breath. I still don't know if I can trust him. But as I looked into his face. I wanted to trust him. He looked so earnest and sincere. Not the face of someone who would lie and cheat.

'Listen, Luke, you have no idea what I went through. How I felt. Because yes, I did feel that we had something special and I thought you felt it too and that's why I trusted you and . . . well . . . you betrayed that trust. I wish for just two minutes you could have been in my shoes and known how it felt . . .'

'I know. I know. My fault. Stupid. It's because I don't want to hurt anyone, but in the end I hurt everyone, including myself. But what I wanted to say was . . . I've learned my lesson. Could we . . . do you think you could give me a second chance?'

'But why now? It's been months since we've seen each other.'

'Well, you made it very clear at the time that I wasn't welcome in your life. But I haven't stopped thinking about you, honestly I haven't, and I just about thought I'd got you out of my mind. And then there you were at the bus stop last week and I realised that all the same old feelings were still there. I couldn't kid myself that I was over you.'

Me too, I thought. As he continued to look at me, I felt like leaning forward and kissing him. He was like a magnet, pulling, pulling . . . I made myself resist. I wanted to be completely certain that he was on the level this time. No secrets. No complications. I couldn't bear to get so hurt again.

'I . . . I . . . It's half-term now . . .'

'I know and there's so many things I want to do and places I'd love to take you. There's a great exhibition . . . Oh. I . . . I was just assuming that you're not with anyone at the moment, but of course, you might be. Sorry. Is there? Have you got a boyfriend at the moment?'

For a moment, I considered telling him about Ollie, but what was there to tell? He wasn't my boyfriend, and after the fiasco in the limo the other night, even though he'd apologised, I wasn't sure if I wanted to see him again.

'No. No one at the moment, but we're going down to Cornwall tomorrow for half-term. Mum and Dad are already there. How about I think about what you've said while I'm away?'

Luke looked disappointed but he nodded. 'OK. Sure. It's your call.'

I squeezed his hand and he smiled.

'No secrets?' I asked. 'No acting weird? No complications? If we do get back together, I'd want everything out in the open.'

'Absolutely,' he said and looked more hopeful. 'I promise.'

I looked around. The café and bar were beginning to fill up with people who had come for the evening's performance in the theatre at the back of the centre. 'How about a walk?'

Luke looked at his watch. 'Sure. A quick one. I'm on shift at the restaurant tonight. They're short-staffed so Dad hauled me in.'

'OK. So walk me home. My brother Paul, who is usually Mr

Liberal, has suddenly assumed the role of Mr Strict, so he'll be very happy if I get back a bit earlier.'

'Sure,' said Luke.

On the walk home he took my hand and we talked easily about general things. It was as if he respected the fact that I needed time to think and he wasn't going to push anything by making the conversation too personal. As we walked up Archway Road, I couldn't help but think how different my journey home this evening was compared to the night before. I felt like I was in my world, on my territory and being with Luke felt completely natural. Last night had felt as if I had been transported to another planet, with the theatre, the limo, the mini-bar and Mr Ollie 'Suave' Axford. I smiled to myself when a white limo like the one I'd ridden in cruised past. Already it was like something that had happened in another lifetime.

When we reached my road and front gate, Luke glanced at his watch again. 'Better get going to the restaurant or Dad'll kill me,' he said.

'OK. So I'll call when we're back.'

'Or while you're down there. It would be great to hear from you whenever. Whenever you're ready, TJ.'

And then he pulled me to him and held me, and it felt like he'd wanted to do it for a long time. I pulled back and turned my face up to his so that he knew that I was feeling the same and he leaned down and kissed me. Tiny sparks of electricity shot through me. It was exactly how I remembered. Marshmallow and chocolate melting . . . melting . . . No reminders to soak paintbrushes. No inner voices arguing with each other.

Only outer voices! It was Luke who pulled back first and looked around.

'TJ!' repeated Paul from the front door.

'TJ!' called Ollie from the open door of the white limo that had just drawn up outside our house. 'And this is?'

Luke looked at me and then at Paul and then at Ollie.

Ollie looked at me then at Luke then at Paul.

Paul looked at Ollie then Luke and then me.

I looked at the open front door and, like a coward, ran for it.

E-mail: **Inbox (1)**
To: babewithbrains@psnet.co.uk
From: leilaferrin@fastmail.com
Date: 26th May
Subject: Top Tip

Hi TJ,
My top tip for writing is: Never give up. Persevere through rejection and tough times and it will pay off in the end – a tip which I apply to my life as well as my writing.
Hope this finds you well, and good luck with it all.

Leila Ferrin.

## Chapter 10

# Relationship Rollercoaster

The long drive down to Cornwall was a blessing. It gave me time to think. And Paul time to tease me like mad. He thought Ollie turning up just when I was mid-snog with Luke was hysterical.

'If you could have seen your face,' he said, as we drove down the A303. 'It was a picture.'

'Well, I'm glad someone found it entertaining,' I said.

After I'd taken refuge inside last night, Paul said that neither Luke nor Ollie had hung about for long. Apparently Ollie had got out of the car (carrying a bunch of flowers, no less) and gone to speak to Luke. Paul couldn't hear exactly what was said, but Ollie soon got back in the car and Luke stormed off down the road.

Later that evening, when I'd calmed down and my breathing had gone back to normal, I'd picked up my e-mails. There was one from Leila Ferrin saying persevere through the bad times. I thought I should apply that philosophy to Luke so I tried to phone him at the restaurant. Whoever picked up the phone said he was working and couldn't talk. It could have been his dad, it could have been one of the other waiters acting on Luke's instructions not to take calls. I felt really bad about my reaction earlier. I had just panicked. My Minnie the Mouse sub-persona had taken over and taken the coward's way out. And then I'd regretted it. I'm not a coward. Not normally. I just didn't know what to do or say. Later in the evening, I tried Luke's mobile. It was switched off. And I tried again a few times this morning before we left but still no luck. I thought about texting him, but changed my mind as I wanted to talk to him in person.

As we drove along, I texted Izzie, Nesta, Lucy and Hannah to bring them up to date, then gazed out of the window at the passing fields and rolling hills that told us we were out of London. The weather had cleared since last night and it looked like it was going to be a gloriously hot day. As I stared up at the blue sky, I replayed the earlier part of the evening with Luke over and over again in my mind. Luke and I did have something amazing. I really wanted to make it work and, even though the end of the evening had turned out disastrously, in one way it proved to me how these sorts of things could happen. It made me think that I had judged Luke too harshly in the past. I believed now that he hadn't meant to hurt me and he hadn't meant to hurt Nesta. It was just a case of bad timing, just as it had been with Ollie showing up around the same time that Luke came back into my life. If I had met Ollie just after Christmas we could have gone out, broken up, gone out and broken up several times over by now. All those months I didn't have any boyfriends, then, as luck would have it, I meet Ollie a week before I bump into Luke again. Bad, *bad* timing, but I would explain to Luke that he was the one I wanted to be with. I wasn't two-timing him. Hopefully he'd understand. If anyone *should* understand, it was him.

I hadn't called Ollie yet even though he'd tried again to call me this morning. I was still working out what I wanted to say. I had his number down in Cornwall so I knew that I could call him and apologise there. I was going to tell him that I hadn't purposely kept anything back from him about Luke because up until that evening there was nothing going on. And then I'd explain that Luke and I were (hopefully) going to get back together. I hoped that Ollie and I could be friends and that he'd understand and not think that I was a scheming, conniving love rat.

After cruising down the A303 for about an hour, Paul turned off the road into a service station. 'Got to get some petrol,' he said. 'So if you need the Ladies, now is the time and, while you're there, get some chocolate supplies.'

As Paul filled the car up, I went and got a few things from the shop inside, then got Mojo out of the back of the car and went and sat on a grassy verge outside the café area where I dialled Luke's mobile. This time, he picked up.

'Oh Luke, hi! It's TJ.'

'Yes. I know who it is,' he said. His voice sounded cold.

'About last night . . .'

'Yes. You made your point. Quite a set-up.'

'Set-up? What do you mean?'

'Earlier. When we were at Jackson's Lane, you said you'd love for me to feel what it was like to be hurt the way that you were. To be two-timed. Well, mission accomplished. Well done. I wouldn't have thought revenge was exactly your style, but I guess I had it coming.'

'No . . . Luke, it wasn't like that.'

'No? What about when I asked if you were with anyone at the moment. You said you weren't. So who was the guy in the limo, then? You don't need to tell me. I asked him and he told me that you'd been dating.'

'No, but we're not . . .'

'Look, I'm not stupid, TJ. Go on, go ahead. Say *all* the stuff that I said to you. It's not serious with him, etc, etc. You're the one I want, etc., etc. Go on, get your own back. I hope you're enjoying it.'

'No, Luke, listen please . . . About Ollie . . .'

'No, you listen. OK, I walked right into it. I got what I deserved. I said I was sorry, but you got me anyway. So now we're equal. I don't want to play games, TJ. And contrary to what you might think, I did really care about you.'

'But . . .'

He didn't give me a chance to say anything. 'Stick with your rich boyfriend,' he said. 'Maybe he doesn't mind girls who play head games.'

And then he hung up!

I felt like I'd been punched in the stomach. So much for perseverance paying off. I felt so mad I wanted to kick something.

'Arrrghhhhhh,' I cried.

Mojo, who was always eager to join in whatever I was doing let out a loud howl. '*Awooohhhh.*'

'Exactly, Mojo,' I said. 'Ablooming*woooooooh.*'

'You all right, love?' asked a middle-aged lady who was going into the service station.

'Oh yes, fine,' I said. 'Just stubbed my toe.'

She gave me a strange look and carried on her way.

'Hey, TJ, come on,' called Paul from the car. 'Best get going if we're to be there for supper.'

For the next couple of hours we drove along listening to the radio, each of us locked in our thoughts and private worlds. I didn't want to discuss my feelings with Paul because I was stunned at Luke's reaction. It was totally unreasonable. He'd thought the worst possible thing about me. Not only that I was seeing someone else, but that I would flaunt it in front of him for revenge. As if! Well, that killed any romantic notion that he somehow knew the real me. I would *never* do anything so calculated, and if he thought I could then he could stuff it. I wasn't into playing games. And he hadn't even given me a chance to explain my side of the story. Pfff. There was no hope for us as a couple. If a boy wasn't even prepared to listen, then what chance did we have? None.

As we drove further down south, the countryside began to open up and became greener. Paul and I began to chat more and for a while it took my thoughts off boys and what complications they caused. We drove on through Exeter, down past Plymouth, across the Saltash Bridge and on to one of the B-roads leading to the Rame Peninsula.

'Not much longer,' said Paul as we drove down a road with

high hedgerows on both sides. 'In fact, we've done good time. Four and a half hours. We should be there before five.'

He turned a corner and suddenly we were out in the open again and could see where we were.

'Wow!' I gasped when I saw the panoramic view in front of us.

'Woweekazowee,' said Paul, and pulled the car over so that we could take it all in.

The countryside in front of us was spectacular. A perfect scene. A perfect day with not a cloud in the blue, blue sky. To our right and ahead as far as the eye could see, was the ocean – glistening silver blue in the late afternoon light. Miles and miles of it along an unspoilt coastline that stretched out in front of us until, in the far distance, it reached a part of the landscape that jutted out into the sea. To our left were rolling hills, valleys and fields of green and honey colours.

'This is absolutely stunning,' I said. 'It's like a painting.'

Paul consulted his map then pointed out to the sea. 'That's Whitsand Bay along there, and that hill with the little church on top in the far distance is probably Rame Head.'

'Fanbloomingtabulous,' I said.

'Exactly,' said Paul as he started up the car again.

We drove on down through winding lanes, through a small village called Millbrook, and once we were through it, we found the landmarks that Mum had told us to look out for. Left at the school at the top of the hill, two miles through woodland, two big rock boulders after the turn off to Anderton, and then take a left on a road with an orchard on your left and a field with horses on your right.

We carried on down the sandy lane as instructed, took a left at the bottom and then found ourselves in a private bay.

It was beautiful. A quiet inlet of water with one boat bobbing about in the low tide. The only sound was the water lapping gently. On the land in front was Rose Harbour Cottage and there, in a deckchair on the lawn leading down to the bay, was Dad. It looked like he was asleep as he had his Panama hat over his face. He looked the picture of perfect peace.

Mum came running out when she heard the car. She looked much more rested than when they left last week and so pleased to see us. She took our bags from the boot and ushered us inside the cottage.

'It used to be a coaching inn,' said Mum as she gave us the tour and led us through the forty-foot, low-beamed living room and into a vast open kitchen with a little conservatory off to the right. The whole place smelled of woodsmoke, as if hundreds of log fires had been burned there. 'And I think this part was built later.'

Upstairs on two floors were four spacious bedrooms, each with double windows, a window seat and a view of the ocean. There were two large bathrooms and, at the back in an outhouse, there was a snooker room, complete with table. There was a garden with a pond and barbecue area at the side, as well as the lawn at the front. Fabulous, I thought. I could see that we were going to have a great week here.

After tea and sandwiches, I went up to my room on the first floor to unpack. As I was putting things away in the pine wardrobe, my mobile rang. For a moment my stomach turned over as I thought it might be Luke calling to apologise or talk things over.

'Hi,' said Ollie's voice.

'Oh. Hi,' I said. 'I'm glad you called. I wanted to talk to you. Er . . . About last night. I want to explain.'

'No, me first. I want to explain about what happened in the limo on the way back from the circus the other night. I'm sorry I pushed things along too fast. That's why I was there waiting for you last night. I'm really sorry. I got carried away and . . . well, sorry.'

'You're sorry? Oh right. Yes, of course, the limo!' I said. I'd been so busy thinking about what I was going to say to him about running away last night and about Luke that I'd completely forgotten about the groping incident. 'It's cool. Apology accepted.'

'Really?'

'Yes. Forgiven. Forgotten.'

'Wow, TJ, you really are something. Excellent.'

'And I wanted to say that I'm sorry too. You know . . . for diving inside last night when I saw you. Sorry.'

Ollie laughed. 'That guy didn't seem too happy to see me either,' he said. 'Who was he?'

'Luke. No. I guess he wasn't too happy.'

'And Luke is?'

'Old boyfriend. Unfinished business.'

'Still unfinished?'

'Nope, I think we've pretty well got that one wrapped up now.'

'Fab, so we can hang out,' said Ollie. 'And I promise no more funny stuff. You on your way down to Cornwall?'

'No. I'm here already.'

'Excellent. I'll be down tomorrow, so see you at your cottage?'

'Yeah. Sure,' I said. Why not? I thought. Luke has just blown me out. Why shouldn't I see Ollie? 'And . . . you're not mad or anything about last night?'

'Nope,' said Ollie. 'It's not as if we were married or anything. We're young, we're free, we're single! And a girl like you, I expect competition.'

Hah! I thought. If only you knew my track record (or lack of it).

'Yes, it really is difficult some days,' I said. 'I have to fight the boys off.'

'Me too. Or girls that is in my case.' Ollie laughed. 'It's hard being as drop-dead gorgeous and desirable as I am.'

I laughed, but I hoped he was joking.

'OK, so we're cool,' I said.

'Yep. We're cool,' said Ollie.

Wow, I thought as I clicked my phone shut. Relationships really are a rollercoaster. On-off, on-off, up-down, up-down. But did I make a mistake saying I'd see him? No. Why shouldn't I? Luke had just made his feelings very clear, and if he wasn't prepared to talk *and* listen, what could I do? I wasn't going to spend the week pining over him. I'd spent too many weeks doing that when I could have been having a life. I'm a free agent. No ties. No commitments, and I have two choices. Sit down here and mope about Luke, who may never want to see me again. Or go out and have some fun with a guy who is great company.

I knew which option I was going to take.

Texts to TJ from the girls about the
Luke/Ollie situation:

GIVE OLLIE ANOTHER GO. *Lucy*

FIND A NEW BOY, BET THERE ARE LOADS DOWN THERE. *Nesta*

DON'T GIVE UP ON LUKE. THINK HE OVERREACTED COS LIKES U V. MUCH. KEEP AN OPEN MIND. AND DON'T FORGET OUR MSN CHAT ROOM! *Izzie*

THANKS A LOT, GUYS. NOW I AM REALLY CONFUSED! *TJ*

# Chapter 11

# Half-term Hols

'So what's it like?' asked Izzie when I called her on Monday evening.

'Amazing,' I replied. '*Le Anglaisie* paradise. I love it down here. You've got to come down some time.'

'How's your dad?'

'Good. He looks a lot better. He's not venturing too far from the cottage, but he's happy enough just hanging out in the front garden or watching one of the old movies we found in the TV cabinet. The cottage looks right out on the water and is so peaceful. What have you guys been up to? I sooo wish you were all here. I miss you like mad.'

'Oh, same old, same old,' Izzie replied. 'I wish I was with you too. Nesta and William are inseparable. They went to Hampton Court today with Lucy and Tony and they did invite me along, but no way was I going to go and be the sad singleton. Can you imagine a day out watching those guys fawning over each other? No thanks. Vomitous.'

'I thought Tony was revising for his exams?'

'Yeah, he is most of the time so Lucy will be around tomorrow and later in the week. I don't mind that much. I've got loads to do. I went over to see Ben and the boys from the band today. We went over some new material. Have you seen Ollie?'

'Yes. Today. Paul went back to Bristol last night as he's got a decorating job, so Mum and Dad are really pleased that I know someone down here who can show me around. That way, they can relax and be close to the house and not worry about me getting bored. It's been amazingly hot down here. Everyone says it's like August weather. We've been to some fabtastic places already and I've taken a ton of photos to show you.'

'And is Ollie Wollie behaving?'

'Not a wandering hand in sight.'

'Cool. Keep me updated and don't forget our MSN! I've set it up and I'm the only one who's been in it so far! I've spoken to Lucy and Nesta and we've agreed that for the rest of the half-term we'll go in there at precisely six o'clock every day for a proper catch-up. Be there or be square.'

'Will do.'

After I'd hung up, I checked in with Izzie in the chat room but we'd already said most of what we wanted on the phone so I didn't stay on too long. I did promise that I'd send her some pics though so I went through the ones I'd taken on Mum's digital camera.

Ollie had shown up after breakfast this morning in a bright turquoise Beetle car and, after I'd introduced him to Mum and

Dad, he told me that I was going to be a tourist for the week and he was going to be my guide. He drove me all over the peninsula to give me an overview and it was totally amazing. On one side were the twin villages of Kingsand and Cawsand. They were small fishing villages with cobbled backstreets and a maze of pretty-coloured cottages painted in pink, yellow and blue. There was one road that wound its way through the villages and it was so narrow that there was barely enough room for one car. I loved it. In each village there was a bay that was easy to get to so there were lots of families with kids splashing in the water and enjoying the unseasonably hot weather.

On the other side of the peninsula was Whitsand Bay, where Paul and I had stopped on Saturday afternoon. Ollie took me to a café called the View, which was on top of the cliff up there. It was so named because the outlook from the picnic tables at the front was stunning: just ocean and sky as far as the eye could see. It was completely different to the other side of the penninsula as it was more rugged and unspoiled and people could only get down the cliff side to the beach via a narrow, dusty path through boulders and shrubs.

After Whitsand Bay, we drove down to a place called Cremyl where there was a pub and a foot ferry that took people over to Plymouth. Near there were acres of parkland spread out on a slope overlooking Plymouth, and at the top of a hill stood a grand old house called Mount Edgecumbe that was open to the public.

Ollie was the perfect gentleman all day. Held my hand. Kissed my cheek. No funny business at all, and I began to wonder if I'd imagined the octopus incident in the limo up in London.

The biggest revelation, however, was when he took me to see

his house. I thought it would be like one of the houses in Kingsand village, only maybe a little bigger. Hah! More like a palace. He lives in a place called Barton Hall and you have to drive through huge wrought iron gates and up a long lane past trees to get there and, when you do, wow! It's not big, it's enormous! Like a posh old hotel. It has several reception rooms, a library, loads of bedrooms (I lost count), tennis courts, a swimming pool and his dad has a studio down by a lake at the back. The whole place was decorated beautifully – every room like a page out of one of Nesta's mum's interior magazines, with lovely antiques and huge vases full of gorgeous flowers.

His dad was up in London, but I met his mum, who is blonde and beautiful, and I saw pictures of his sister Lia, who is a year younger than me. Like her mum, she is also very pretty. I hoped I'd get to meet her later on in the week as when we were up at the house she was out somewhere with her boyfriend, Squidge. Ollie told me that Lia had changed from a school in London to a local one because she loved the area so much and wanted to be at home. I asked why he hadn't done the same, but he said that he liked being in London too much and would miss his mates.

I also met the family pets: Max and Molly, two gorgeous red setters, Ug, the Vietnamese pot-bellied pig, and the latest addition, Fish, the ginger kitten. Ollie told me that Fish followed Max and Molly everywhere and thought that he was a red setter too. I thought it must be very confusing for poor Fish, not only thinking he was a dog but having to answer to the name Fish!

'You have very strange pets,' I said.

'Thank you,' said Ollie.

'Why did you call your poor cat Fish?'

'Not my idea. Squidge's mate Mac named him. Apparently he used to have a cat called Rover.'

'Yeah,' I said. 'Kind of follows.'

'All Lia's mates are mad,' said Ollie.

I thought they sounded like fun. It made me realise that I was missing mine even though it had only been three days since I last saw them, which is why I'd called Izzie for a long natter.

**Tuesday 6 p.m.**

**TJ:** Hi guys. S'me. Been exploring with Ollie at old house called Mount Edgecumbe today. Fab. So many interesting paintings and antiques to look at.

**Izzie:** Blarrgghh. Sounds v. boring. Heard from Luke?

**TJ:** Nope. Sad that he and I aren't on speaking terms, because exploring old houses and imagining who'd lived there and what they were like is one of his favourite things, too. I made myself put him out of my mind, though. I was there with Ollie and had to stop comparing them.

**Izzie:** Yep. I agree. Love the one you're with. Which in my case is no one. Boo hoo.

**Nesta:** How's the snog scale with O?

**Izzie:** And any spare decent boys down there in case I ever go there?

**TJ:** O kissed me properly before he dropped me off at the cottage. I can tell that he's making a big effort to hold back and not be pushy. Still not sure what I feel about him, though.

**Nesta:** Look on it all as good practice. It's good for your confidence to flirt and spend time with boys who aren't the great love of your life, as you learn something from everyone.

**TJ:** What u all be up to?

**Lucy:** Hanging out with Tony. Movies. Mooching.

**Nesta:** Hanging out with William. Movies. Mooching.

**Izzie:** God help me. Come home, TJ. All is forgiven.

**Wednesday 6 p.m.**

**Nesta:** Hi guys. How are you all?

**Lucy:** Fabola.

**Izzie:** Been down Camden with Lucy. What you bin up 2, TJ?

**TJ:** O and I got the foot ferry over to Plymouth today. Cool harbour there. Also an aquarium but there was a huge queue for that so we just mooched about the shops and sat about outside cafés, drinking Cokes and watching the boats and the world go by. Felt like holiday time. Sun shining. O is great company. Wonder why I think about grumpy old Luke when a boy like Ollie is interested in me. I'm starting to like him more and more.

**Nesta:** Be careful. I still think that boy is a player!

**Lucy:** Don't worry, TJ. You're not stupid. Enjoy. It's fab weather up here. Hot, hot, hot.

**TJ:** Here too. Lovely jubbly.

**Thursday 6 pm.**

**TJ:** Oh God. Iz, Luce, Nesta are you there?

**Izzie:** Only me. Lucy and Nesta out with the boys somewhere. Tell me all.

**TJ:** I think that Ollie has put a spell on me as I can't stop thinking about him and Luke is beginning to fade into the distance. I even turned my mobile off as I'd been keeping it on all day in case Luke rang, but as the week has gone on, I don't know if I care. I realised that I don't even know Luke that well. We haven't actually spent much time together talking, not the way that Ollie and I have in the last few days. All I know about Luke is that he's into history, wants to be an actor, has a strict dad and . . .

**Izzie:** When he looks into your eyes, your stomach lurches and when he kisses you, you turn to jelly. You might have forgotten but I haven't.

**TJ:** Yeah, but even the memory of that is beginning to fade. Ollie is taking over.

**Izzie:** Hhhmmm.

**TJ:** What's that supposed to mean?

**Izzie:** Means . . . hhmmm.

**TJ:** That's no help!

**Izzie:** Sorry. Feeling sleepy. It's sooo hoooot up here . . . Look TJ, don't worry. You don't have to make up your mind today. You can decide later. For now, just enjoy being down there.

On Friday morning, Ollie drove us along the Whitsand coastline then out towards Liskard.

'Where are we going?' I asked.

'Surprise,' he said.

After about five minutes, he turned off the main road and the car bumped up a dusty lane to a car park area under some trees.

We got out and walked towards what looked like a small zoo.

'Owl sanctuary,' said Ollie, grinning. 'It's one of my favourite places.'

It soon became one of mine too. We paid three pounds each to a man in a little shed and then set off into the sanctuary.

There were large cages on either side of a walkway and inside each one were different species of owls staring out at us. Barn owls, tawny owls, snowy owls, Siberian Eagle owls. All sorts, all sizes. They were so funny. All of them had beautiful feathers, sharp beaks and some had the most vivid, wide orange or yellow eyes, but what made me laugh about them was their expressions. Some of them looked sooooo haughty, others looked sooooo cross and others looked stoned out of their heads and like they were having such a hard time keeping their heavy-lidded eyes open that they were going to fall asleep and drop off their perch at any moment.

'That one looks like our PSHE teacher, Miss Watkins, when she's not pleased with our homework,' I said, as a tawny owl regarded me with utter disdain. It blinked its eyes and turned its head away as if it was so bored looking at me it could no longer bear it.

'I know,' said Ollie. 'They're hysterical, aren't they? I think owls must be my favourite bird.'

'A while back,' said the keeper, who had come out of his shed and was walking along behind us, 'everyone wanted one. It was after the Harry Potter books came out. He's got one, hasn't he?'

'A snowy owl,' I said.

'That's it,' said the keeper. 'Anyway, parents were calling from all over the country. Oo, my Nigel has got to have a snowy owl for Christmas. Oo, my Arabella has to have one for her birthday. Not from me, I told 'em. See, I know what's involved looking after an owl. They're not toys. A lot of kids that got 'em from other places soon lost interest after a few weeks, and who was supposed to feed and look after the poor thing then, eh? We've had a few brought here that were abandoned after some spoiled kid had 'ad enough and realised that owls don't like to be cuddled.'

Ollie looked sheepish for a moment. 'I wanted one when I was eight,' he whispered when the keeper had moved on. 'Dad wouldn't let me have one, though, as I think he knew that they take some looking after. At the time I was so upset as I imagined that the owl would fly to my school in London with post from my mum and dad, but that's only in the books and movies, isn't it?'

'Guess so,' I said. 'I read the books when I was eight, too. I wanted a dragon and even phoned a load of pet shops to see if anyone had them. I thought they were real.'

At the end of our visit, the keeper brought out four baby owls and put them in my hands. They were so gorgeous, like little balls of fluff, and Ollie took a picture of them. He went totally soppy over them and held them for ages. Luke was so wrong about Ollie, I thought, as I watched him stroke the baby owls. Calling him 'my rich boyfriend' as if he showed off about it or something. He wasn't like that at all. So yes, he lived in a fab place, but he wasn't all swanky about it. In fact, when we got back in the car, he told me that what impresses him most in the whole world are natural things like animals or birds or fish. As we drove away, I got the feeling that I'd just met another of Ollie's sub-personalities. A gentle one with a great love of nature.

After the sanctuary, we drove back towards Whitsand where, after a short distance, Ollie turned off the main road again.

'Where to this time?' I asked. 'Another surprise?'

'Lunch,' he said and pointed down to the right.

'Wow. Now that looks like it's straight out of Harry Potter,' I said as a grey stone castle, complete with turrets, came into view.

'Whitsand Bay Hotel,' he said. 'I thought we could get a bite there and then go down to the beach.'

I nodded. 'Sounds great.' I felt so happy. I was falling in love with the area. And after seeing how sweet Ollie was with the owls, I was falling in love with him.

Already I was having fantasies about owning a cottage down here when I was older. I could come down to write or paint. Of course, all my friends would be here too with their various partners and kids and dogs, cats, goats and chickens, and we'd sit and watch the sunrises and sunsets and laugh and live happily ever after.

The inside of the hotel reeked of history, with oak-panelled walls, old paintings, parquet flooring and huge floor-to-ceiling windows overlooking a garden planted with shrubs and palm plants on terraces that led down to the sea.

Ollie ordered cheese and tomato sandwiches and Cokes from the bar then found us a table outside as the sun was shining brightly and we didn't want to miss a moment of it. I sat back in my chair and closed my eyes to soak up the rays.

'This place has to be as close to heaven as you could find,' I said after the waiter had brought us our sandwiches. 'Not too busy or touristy. The most divine views. I don't know. There's something about the place. I feel so happy here. Peaceful.'

Ollie nodded. 'That's what Mum and Dad say. That's why they moved here. And Lia. She loves it too.'

'I can see why,' I said, and pulled my phone out. When I turned it on, it bleeped that I had a message waiting.

'Oh, leave it,' said Ollie. 'Whatever it is, it can probably wait. I'm going back to London this evening so we have to make the most of our last few hours here together.'

I smiled back at him. 'Yeah. Later,' I said, and put the phone away. I had promised that I'd let Mum know what time I'd be back, but it felt like nothing mattered. The sun was shining. The sea in front of us was twinkling with silver sparkles. The world felt at peace.

After we'd eaten our lunch, we went for a walk on the beach in front of the hotel. We held hands and paddled in the sea and then lay on our backs in the sand for a while and talked and cuddled. I turned to look at Ollie's handsome face and traced his profile with my index finger.

'I feel very happy,' I said.

He caught my finger with his lips and kissed it. 'Me too, TJ Watts. I think you are one of the coolest girls I have ever met.'

And then he leaned over and kissed me on the lips.

When Ollie kissed me this time, it felt real. Like he meant it. And for me there was no more thinking about his technique or paintbrushes or phone calls I had to make later. I felt totally in the present and only aware of the sensation of his lips on mine.

Around four, Ollie dropped me back at the cottage as he had to go and catch the train back to London. Plus I had promised that I'd go for a walk with Dad and Mojo before supper.

After a goodbye snogathon in the car and promises to see

each other in London, I got out and pretty much skipped down the lane to Rose Harbour. It had been the best day ever and I was feeling really good about being with Ollie. I haven't felt this happy in ages, I thought, as I went to open the front door.

It wouldn't open.

I tried again but the door was locked.

I knocked but no answer.

I peered through the window, but couldn't see any sign of Mum or Dad. Only Mojo at the window, barking his objection at being left inside. Where could they be, I wondered? Maybe Mum had left the key for me in our secret hiding place under the pot of geraniums and then gone into the village for supplies, but then why hadn't they taken Mojo? Maybe Marie had come over from Devon and taken them off somewhere? But no, she wouldn't have. I'd spoken to her on Monday night and I knew she had to work and make up for the time she had off when she was up in London after Dad's stroke.

I found the key and let myself in to the cottage. Then I got my phone out and switched it on to see if Mum had left a message on my voicemail.

She had.

Three.

'TJ. Your dad's not good. I'm taking him to the hospital in case he's had another stroke. Keep your phone switched on so that I can get in touch if there's any news. I'll call as soon as I can.'

'TJ. Oh God, where are you? Why haven't you got your phone on?'

'TJ. I'm at the hospital now. The doctors are doing what they can. Here's the number of the ward. 01752 33546, ward 14. Call when you get this message.

Suddenly the day felt cold. My happy mood disappeared like water down a drain.

# Chapter 12

# All Mates Together

**Mum wouldn't hear** of me going to the hospital.

'There's nothing you can do. I'll call as soon as there are any developments.'

'But . . . what happened? Is he going to be all right?'

'Too early to tell, love. Are you still with your friend Ollie?'

'No. He's gone.'

'Then take Mojo out for a walk, take your phone with you and this time keep it switched on.'

'But what exactly happened?'

'He . . . Oh . . . got to go, the doctor's come out. I'll call later.'

She hung up. I felt like I'd been punched in the stomach. I stared out of the window at the sea for a while. Hell, I thought. Heaven and hell. All in one day. I didn't know what to do with myself. I felt numb. I didn't want to eat. Didn't want to drink. I flicked on the TV but couldn't concentrate. I checked my watch. Four-thirty. Too early for MSN. I thought about phoning the girls up in London, but if I left a message then they might phone back when Mum was trying to get through. Best to leave the line free. And anyway, what could they say? Or do? Nothing. And I couldn't call Hannah in South Africa. It would cost a fortune.

'Come on,' I said to Mojo. 'Let's go for a run.'

Mojo wagged his tail in agreement. He clearly thought it was an excellent idea.

I stuffed my phone into my back pocket and ran down to Cremyl, through the Italian gardens at Mount Edgecumbe, and then followed the footpath through the woods and along the coast. It felt good to run. It took my mind off the dark thoughts that were threatening to take over. SP Cassandra, prophetess of doom, had taken over. I could hear her moaning on in the back of my head. *Woe, woe* . . . Get lost, you creep, I told her. Dad's going to be all right. I know he is. He's going to be all right.

Mojo ran ahead of me and then back to make sure I was keeping up and then off he'd charge ahead again as we panted our way through the woods and over towards Kingsand. Once there, I ran down through the back lanes of the village and then on to the main street through into Cawsand. It was as if I couldn't stop. The pound pound pound of my feet on the ground was stomping out bad thoughts. I ran down into the square at Cawsand then turned left on the beach area, and there at last I stopped to catch my breath. The beach was occupied by a few families still enjoying the late afternoon sun, so I scanned the area to try and find a quiet spot where I could be alone. Over to the left, there were several moored boats and behind there was an area where the beach looked stony. No one was sitting there. I made my way over and sat down on the gravel behind a large boulder.

Once I knew that I was hidden from the rest of the beach by a boat, I let the tears flow. Mojo looked at me with alarm and put his paws up on my shoulders and tried to lick my face.

I buried my face in my arms and sobbed. I hate this feeling, I thought, hate it hate it hate it. Not nice. Please, please God, let Dad be all right. The scare a few weeks ago was bad enough, but I thought he was getting better. Was this how it was going to be now that he was getting older? Scare after scare? Or was this it? The end? And Mum's getting older. When would Mum die? Oh God. She was going to die sometime, too. On and on I sobbed. I didn't want them to die. I didn't want anyone I knew to die.

'Hey,' said a voice up to my right. 'Are you OK? At least, I can see you're *not* OK, but is there anything I can do? Anyone I get for you?'

I looked up and saw that a girl, about my age, with short dark hair, was standing by one of the boats and staring down at me. She had a sweet, pixie face, was very pretty and dressed in denim shorts and a pink T-shirt with a silver glitter star on it.

I wiped my nose and my eyes. 'Oh God. No. Sorry. I . . . I didn't think anyone would come over here. I . . . I thought I was safe.'

The girl came and sat down next to me. 'You are safe here. I'll go away if you want but . . . I can stay too if you like.'

'Sorry . . .' was all I could say as another wave of tears rose up inside of me. 'I . . . don't . . . seem . . . to . . . be . . . hic . . . able to stop crying.'

The girl put her hand on my arm. 'Hey. Don't be sorry. Sometimes it's good to have a good cry. I'll let you into a secret. That's how I know about this place. It's my place to come and cry.'

'Yours? But why?'

The girl shrugged. 'Oh . . . few reasons. I used to come here when I was little with my family.' She pointed at the families playing a distance away on the sandier side of the beach. 'That was us. Happy families. Mum died when I was nine. So I come here partly to remember her and the times we had here when she was alive and partly to blub my head off when I want to. Don't laugh, but I like it best when it's really stormy, like *really* throwing it down and I can sit here and cry and watch the ocean and the rain and feel like the whole world is crying with me. It's very therapeutic.'

'Yeah. Sounds it.'

'So what's the matter?'

I took a deep breath and let the last sob subside. 'My dad's not well. He's at the hospital and I'm scared . . . he's . . . going . . . to die . . .' The tears started again.

'Hey, hey,' said the girl. 'I understand. You don't have to give me details if you don't want. I know what it's like. Like you're raw inside.'

'Yeah,' I sniffed. 'Raw and numb at the same time, and . . . I feel like every part of me is being stretched too far and it . . . it . . . sob . . . hurts.'

The girl put her arm round me and gave me a hug. 'We all know that people die,' she said. 'But no one's ever ready for it.'

'Yeah,' I sniffed again. Poor girl. Her mum actually had died and that only made it seem more possible that Dad might. I could feel I was going to start blubbing again.

'Want me to leave?' asked the girl.

'No. Not unless you have somewhere to go.'

'Nope. Nothing urgent. I mean, my dad could probably find me a million things to do if he wanted which is actually why I'm hiding down here. He runs the shop up in village. Have you been there?'

I shook my head. 'No, but my mum probably has, I think. Um . . . I'm TJ by the way. Least, my friends call me that.'

'Cool name,' said the girl. 'My friends call me Cat. Cat Kennedy. Short for Catherine.'

'Suits you,' I said. 'You look a bit like a cat.'

Cat smiled. She seemed nice. Easy going. I was just about to say something else when my phone rang. I quickly answered it.

It was Mum.

'TJ, love?'

'Yes. How is he?'

'He's doing fine. Indigestion,' said Mum. 'So false alarm.'

'Oh, thank God,' I said. 'So it wasn't another stroke?'

'No, it wasn't. But it's a warning, I think. He really does have to change his diet and keep off the rich food he likes so much.'

'Are you still at the hospital?'

'Yes. The doctors are doing a few more tests to be on the safe side, and of course your father is driving them all mad by telling them what to do and not letting them get on with their jobs, but . . . I guess that's a good sign.'

'Are they going to let him home?'

'We'll be back in an hour or so.'

I beamed at Cat as I clicked my phone shut and let out a deep breath.

'Good news?' she asked.

'He's going to be OK. Oh, God. I must look a right mess. God. I'm so sorry, crying all over you. And nicking your secret place.'

'You're welcome to it,' she said. 'I'm really pleased your dad's going to be OK.'

'Yeah. Mum said that they'll be home in a hour or so.'

'That's great,' said Cat. 'So, I haven't seen you down here before. Where are you from?'

'London. North London. We're staying at Rose Harbour Cottage . . .'

Cat nodded. 'I know it. Oh. So your mum and dad are the doctors?' Then she laughed. 'Sorry. Everyone knows everyone's business down here. Especially when your dad runs the local shop.'

'That's us,' I said. 'I've fallen in love with the place. I want all my mates to come down in the summer if they can as I think Dad wants to rent the cottage where we're staying again. Hey, seeing as you're local, you don't happen to know a good B and B do you? Somewhere my mates could stay in case my brother and sister happen to be visiting the cottage and hogging the spare rooms.'

'Yeah. I know just the place,' said Cat. 'My mate Mac's mum runs one. Actually it's his gran's house. It's a lovely place. Loads of space. Great views. She was really glad when they came down. His gran, that is. I think she was finding the place too big for just her. Anyway, Mac's mum has great taste. She's done the rooms out beautifully. Mac used to live in London, then his parents got divorced and he moved down here with his mum . . . anyway, long story. He didn't like it at first, wanted to be back in London all the time, but he likes it now. Actually he's in London for half-term visiting his dad. God, I'm rambling, aren't I? Sorry. You asked if I knew a good B and B. Yes. Mac's. Wouldn't mind staying there myself. I'll give you the number, and mine too if you like.'

'Thanks. That would be brill.'

'You could check it out before you go back if you want. It's not far from Rose Cottage. God. Mac would *love* it if a bunch of London girls came down and stayed there. He's always going on that there's a lack of girls down here. He used to go out with my mate Becca for a while but they broke up. Still friends, though. But yes, if you and your mates came down, Mac would think he'd died and gone to heaven.'

'What are the boys like here? Are there any decent ones? See, my mate Izzie is single at the moment and her horoscope said that she'd find love in the summer.'

Cat laughed. 'Really? Hey. Maybe she'll get it together with Mac. And then we can all be friends. But apart from him, local boys? Well, there's a few. Mac's cute. Not my type . . .'

'What's your type, then?' I asked. After the intensity of the last hour, it felt good to be chatting about boys and normal stuff like I did back home with Izzie, Lucy and Nesta.

'Mine? Hmmmm. I have to admit I do like good-looking boys. I know in the end it doesn't matter, as it's whether they're good company or not that's important, but I am a sucker for a handsome face.'

I laughed. 'I know what you mean.'

'They can be trouble, though,' said Cat. 'Especially the ones who know that they're good-looking. They can mess you around.'

'Tell me about it.' I really liked this girl. She was so easy to talk to. 'Sounds like you're speaking from experience.'

'I guess I am. Like, there's this guy I have an on-off thing with. He's so cute. Like sooooo cute. But good company, too. He's dead bright. But I never know where I am with him. In fact, I've got a feeling that he's seeing someone else at the moment and not telling me about it.'

'Really?'

'Yeah. It's funny because I met him here, too. Right here last summer. This very spot. He came over and chatted me up. I liked him straight away. And now well, we see each other when he's down from school, but this half-term I've only seen him twice and it's like he's distracted so I don't know . . . I feel like something's going on. I think he's two-timing me but then, because he's at school up in London and I'm down here, it's not as if we've made each other promises to be faithful, etc, etc. No point. I know what he's like. His sister warned me that he was a Casanova. It's just I thought that down here, well, you know . . . I thought down here that he was mine.'

Alarm bells had begun to rung when she said this boy came down from school in London. And was a Casanova.

'Why don't you ask him?' I asked.

'No way. That would really scare him off if I came over all possessive. I mean, I know this boy and he's got severe commitment phobia.'

'Er . . . what's his name?'

'Ollie,' said Cat. 'Ollie Axford. He's one of the Axford family. His dad is Zac Axford. Ever heard of him?'

I felt myself wince inside. Outside, I nodded. 'Rock star.'

'That's him. Really nice bloke, though. I've met him. I know his whole family, in fact. Lia, his sister, is one of my best mates. She goes out with Squidge, who was my boyfriend when I was younger, but we broke up and now we're all mates. All mates together. Me, Lia, Becca, Squidge and Mac. Hey TJ . . . Are you OK? You look like you're going to cry again.'

'No,' I said. Bugger bugger bugger, I was thinking. I meet this great girl. I know we could be friends, but how do I tell her that actually *I'm* the one who's seeing her boyfriend. I'm the one that he's two-timing her with. And as for Ollie Axford. I think I may have to kill him.

E-mail: **Inbox (2)**
To: <u>babewithbrains@psnet.co.uk</u>
From: <u>hannahnutter@fastmail.com</u>
Date: 29th May
Subject: Ollie!

My fruity little fruit fly.
Sorry it's been a while, left my phone at Bruce's so only just just seen your last text.

Excooth me? You were being groped in back of car by Ollie Wollie? Er . . . excoooo*oooooth* mee*eeee*? You can't just leave it there. Details darlingus, details. Calling TJ Watts, calling TJ Watts, what on earth are you getting up to over there in Slutville? E-mail back tutto pronto.


Hannahlulu


E-mail: **Inbox (2)**
To: <u>babewithbrains@psnet.co.uk</u>
From: <u>hannahnutter@fastmail.com</u>
Date: 31st May
Subject: *Ou est tu?*


Oi you! *C'est moi, le grand poo.*
Hasta la banana baby. Why have I bin cast so cruelly from your life?

Missing person alert. Where is u gone to my lovely? Oh I

know! Mi forgeti. Tis the half termius and you wos going down to Cornwallus. Oh well. Don't eat too many Cornish pasties . . .

Barbecue happening at Bruce's, so got to go and do scoffie gobs.

Luvvie duvvie wotsits, spik spok soon.
Hannahlulu

PS: Bin thinking about the big quessie. The Big Boss. God. Think the lovely Lucy is right about no creation without un creator. Got to be something or someone over the rainbow and all. And I think that probably like all artists/creators, he/she/it would probably like it if people appreciated his/her/its work. So Nesta is right, too.

Get on and enjoy it. Get down and boogie, baby. There's so much great stuff going on to see, to hear, to feel, taste and touch so let's get on and groove like a groovemeister and dig it, wasps and all. Olé.

PPS: I asked Bruce about God and he said that he is the Chosen One. Sad innit how all boys think that they are God.

PPPS: My mate Confucius, he say he who knows the way is wey hey hey.

XXXXX Squillion love things, and may your flobablobs be mighty!!

## Chapter 13

# Cowardy
# Custard

That evening, after meeting Cat, I didn't even bother trying MSN. Nor did I feel like answering Hannah's e-mails when I checked on the cottage computer. I needed to hear Izzie's voice.

'So why didn't you tell her?' asked Izzie after I'd told her what had happened.

'Don't know. Panic. I froze. I just couldn't do it, Izzie. She'd been so nice to me about Dad and I didn't want her to think that I am a ratfink boyfriend stealer. I can't believe it's happening again. Last year with Luke and Nesta, and now with Cat and Ollie. She'd have hated me if I'd told her.'

'But it wasn't your fault, TJ,' said Izzie. 'You weren't to know that he had a girlfriend down there . . .'

'And God only knows how many up in London. No wonder he was so cool when he saw me snogging Luke before I came down here. Remember he said, "Oh well, it's not as though we're married". I've been such an idiot. Naïve is my middle name. He even told me that one of his sub-personalities was called Casanova, so it's not as if he didn't let me know what he was like. I'm soooo stupid. I should have asked him if he was involved with anyone. It's just that things felt so good between us that I presumed . . . well . . . I presumed that we were an item. Sadly, Cat thought that too.'

'*Not* your fault, TJ. And you mustn't beat yourself up about it. You really mustn't.'

'Stupid and a coward. Cowardy cowardy custard. That's me. A Minnie the Mouse. Part of me didn't tell her that I knew Ollie because I'm a coward and I knew that we're coming back to London on Saturday, and if I don't come down here again I will never have to see her.'

'But all week you've been saying that you wanted us all to come down in the summer? You, me, Lucy and Nesta hanging out down there.'

'Changed my mind,' I said. 'There must be other parts of Cornwall. I'm never coming here again.'

'But you love it down there, you told me.'

'I know. I do. But what about Ollie and Cat . . .?'

'Oh, TJ,' said Izzie. 'If you stay away from a place you like then you really are a coward. And to avoid Cat, a girl who you *like*? You're mad. I bet you she'd understand if you explained it all to her. And what about Ollie? Are you going to see him again?'

'He can take a running jump as far as I'm concerned. He's already texted me to say that he's on his way back up to London and is looking forward to seeing me up there. I haven't replied, though.'

'But as you said yourself, he told you he was a Casanova so he didn't exactly lie to you. He just didn't tell you the whole truth. You can't spend your whole life running away from people or avoiding them because you're afraid of confrontation or what they might think of you.'

'I know,' I groaned. 'Just . . . honestly, Iz, I'm feeling really disillusioned at the moment. Boys. I'm through with all of them. You can't trust any of them. I am going to stay single for the rest of my life. In fact, I will probably become a nun.'

I could hear Izzie laughing at the other end of the phone. 'Ah, so you won't want to know about Luke, then?'

'Luke? What about Luke?'

'Well, if you're through with boys and never want to hang out with one ever again, there's really no point in me telling you.'

'Izzie?'

'Yes, TJ?'

I couldn't see Izzie's face, but I knew she had an almighty great smirk on it. 'If you don't tell me what you know about Luke, Izzie Foster, I will have to . . . have to go and throw myself off the nearest cliff.'

'Ah, but then you'll *never* find out what I have to say . . .'

'IZZIEEEEEEE!'

'OK. OK. Luke has been asking about you.'

'Asking you?'

'No. Not me. Nesta. Well, not Nesta exactly, but Nesta through William. William told Nesta that Luke asked him to find out everything that he could about you and Ollie. And she said that Luke told William that he's really hung up about you and thinks he might have blown it by overreacting last time he saw you. He also made William promise not to tell Nesta any of this, but she knew that he knew something and threatened to dump him if he didn't spill, so he told her everything . . .'

'Wow,' I said. 'That was really good of her because she likes William a *lot*.'

'Yeah, but she knew that he'd give in. He's lucky that she didn't go to Plan B, which was to give him a Chinese burn if he didn't talk. She has her methods, does our Nesta, and isn't one to give up. Anyway, William made Nesta promise not to tell any of us. Ha ha. As if. She was straight on the phone. I think she tried to phone you too, but it was engaged.'

'I was probably talking to Mum,' I said. And then thought, oh no, Luke asking about Ollie? Even though I love Nesta dearly, God only knows what she told William with her big mouth.

'What exactly did Nesta say?'

'She says she didn't tell him anything except that you had only met Ollie recently and it was early days, and she didn't know if you were even going to see him again as you weren't sure if he was your type.'

'Really? Hey, good for her. That's not bad. It leaves it open.'

'Yeah,' said Izzie.

'Cool,' I said.

'Yeah, cool,' said Izzie. 'Sounds to me like you and Luke have some unfinished business.'

'Very possibly,' I said as I thought about our last kiss. Second kiss, actually. Our first kiss last year in our living room in London was disturbed by my parents coming home, and our second kiss was disturbed halfway through by Ollie and Paul. So Luke and I definitely had unfinished business. Of the snogging type.

'Izzie?'

'Yes, TJ?'

'Do you think I am a slut?'

'Definitely.'

'No, really.'

'Yes, really,' said Izzie, but I could hear her laughing. 'Why would you think that?'

'Well, only this lunchtime there was me thinking that Ollie was maybe The One, and last week when I saw Luke I thought he was *definitely* The One. And now that I know that Ollie likes to play the field, I don't think he could possibly be The One for me because I don't think that I could handle feeling strongly about someone and knowing that they were seeing someone else as well. I couldn't do the open relationship thing. I think I'd get too jealous. But he and Luke have shown me that I can feel for more than one person at the same time. I have. I did. I do. Ollie and Luke. It's different with both of them, least I feel different things. Both nice. So does that actually make me the love rat? And not them? I think I'm very confused.'

Izzie was really laughing now. 'Yeah, really confused. Er . . . can you run that by me again?'

'Run what?'

'All that you just said.'

'Oh God no,' I said. 'I can't even remember what I said.'

'Confused,' said Izzie. 'You.'

'Yes. I think that was about the gist of it.'

'Don't worry,' said Izzie. 'Love can be very confusing. It will get clearer. Give it time.'

Izzie is so wise, I thought. 'OK,' I said. 'How long?'

'Oh . . . about three or four . . . hundred years.'

'Thanks a bunch.'

'You're welcome,' said Izzie, and then she started sniggering again.

'Well, I'm glad you find my love life so amusing.'

'Don't worry so much,' said Izzie. 'All you need to do is be true to yourself and honest with everyone else.'

'Right,' I said. Easier said than done, I thought. Be true to myself? Which one of my selves? There are so many people living in my head. All with voices. And all with feelings. And those feelings keep changing every five minutes. I think I am well and truly and completely and utterly bonkers.

'And if you're not true to yourself,' said Izzie, 'the universe will conspire to make you. Least that's what I think. If you try and run away from what you fear then something will happen to make you face your fears. So there. Iz the Oracle has spoken.'

Izzie was always coming out with stuff like that. I think that she may be bonkers too. That is probably why we are such good friends.

'I hear and obey, O wise one,' I said.


On Saturday morning, as Mum packed up our things ready for our return to London, Dad and I took Mojo for a final walk in the woods.

'I want to talk to you about something important,' said Dad as we set off through the fields that led down to Cremyl.

My heart almost stopped – he looked so grave when he said this. Immediately Cassandra, prophetess of doom, raised her head ready to hear the worst as my imagination went into overdrive. Ohgoooooood, said her gloomy voice, he's going to tell you that he hasn't long to live. Woe oh woe oh blooming woe.

Dad put his hand on my shoulder. 'Hey, no need to look so worried.'

'So what is it?'

Dad looked around and gestured at the landscape with his right hand. 'This place. It is wonderful, isn't it?'

Oh no, I thought. I know what's coming. He wants to live here. Last year he and Mum were on about moving to Devon, leaving London. Oh God. I'm not ready to move.

'Er . . . yes. Lovely. Very nice, but . . .'

'Don't worry, TJ, we're not going to leave London. Not yet. Your mother's not ready to retire yet and I'm not ready to leave London forever. I still love living there. No. But maybe there's a compromise that everyone will be happy with. Dr Rollands phoned last night with a proposition that your mum and I are considering carefully, and of course we want to know what you think as well. He's buying a place in France and needs to make some capital, so he's putting Rose Harbour Cottage on the market. He wanted to know if we were interested. What your mother and I thought was that we could have it as a holiday home. I need to slow down a bit, take note of the warning signals my body's been giving me lately, so we thought I'd go part time at the hospital. We'd spend most of the year in London, but summer and the odd weekend down here. Best of both worlds. What do you think?'

'Yes . . . Best of both worlds,' I said.

Izzie was right, I thought, as we walked on and chatted about the cottage. I can't object to something that will be so good for Mum and Dad because I'm a coward. I can't run away from what I fear. If we're going to be down here for summers and the odd weekend, there were two people I was bound to bump into from time to time and I'd have to sort things out with them sooner or later.

Ollie and Cat.

Gulp.

Be true to yourself and honest with everyone else.
Mystic Iz

# Chapter 14

# Coming
# Clean

**I answered Hannah's e-mails** the moment I got home from Cornwall, and put her in the picture. Then it was out the door and off to see Lucy, Nesta and Izzie. I didn't even unpack. It was straight round to Nesta's, where we'd all arranged to meet for a proper catch-up.

Nesta was dying to show the photos she'd taken on her digicam. 'So you can see exactly what I've been up to,' she said.

'You'd be a rubbish travel journalist,' I said as I scrolled through. 'All of these are close-ups of William. None of them show the location.'

Nesta laughed. 'He was the most interesting part of the landscape. Come on, then, show us yours.'

I got my camera out and showed them my pics of the Rame Peninsula, although I'd already e-mailed some of them through from the computer down at the cottage. All of the girls were up for going there in the summer.

'I've asked Mum and Dad already,' said Lucy. 'And they're into the idea as they spent their honeymoon down there and want to go back. Steve and Lal like the idea too.'

'I think Mum and Angus want to go to some château in France this summer, so I don't know if I can come with you,' said Izzie.

'There is room at the cottage,' I said. 'You could come with us and then your mum wouldn't need to worry.'

'Good plan, Batgirl,' said Izzie. 'And then Mum and Angus can go and do their Frenchie thing *sans* teen. She'd probably love that. What about you, Nesta?'

Nesta sighed and draped herself on her bed. 'I don't know if I could bear to be apart from William for too long, and Mum and Dad have been talking about going to Italy for a while so I'll let you know. If William has to go away with his family then of course I'll be down some time.'

'Excellent,' I said. 'I just know you're all going to love it.'

'So what are you going to do about Ollie?' asked Lucy.

'And Cat?' asked Izzie.

'And Luke?' asked Nesta.

'Who?' I asked.

Nesta gave Izzie and Lucy the nod and they grabbed pillows from Nesta's bed and began to beat me with them. I tried my best to grab one and fight back, but I didn't stand a chance.

'Hey, not fair, three against one,' I groaned, as they wrestled me to the floor and Lucy sat on my back.

'We've been giving your situation a lot of consideration while you've been away,' she said, 'and we, the council, have decided that you need to come clean with all of them. Cat, Luke and Ollie.'

'I will. I was going to. Honest.'

'When?' said Izzie.

'Oh . . . some time this week.'

'Do you have their numbers on you?' asked Nesta.

I nodded.

'So do it now,' said Nesta.

'Now? No. I . . . have to think about it. What to say and all that.'

Lucy shook her head. 'The more you think about it, the more scary it will seem. Do it now. Remember my mum's saying, don't put off until tomorrow what you can do today.'

'I can't. You're all here. I can't do it while you're all listening in. You'll make me laugh.'

'Promise we won't,' said Nesta. 'But which one are you going to go for? Ollie or Luke.'

'Luke,' I said. It felt weird coming out with it like that to Nesta, seeing as he was her boyfriend first. I was still worried that it might all turn sour again. 'I . . .I think he wants to be with me. Just me. And so does Ollie, in a way, but not just me – I'd be one on a list and I can't do that.'

'Good,' said Nesta, 'because you're worth more than that. You deserve someone who wants you and you alone. I think it's disrespectful to you to put you on a list, like you're not special enough. And you are. And I think Luke knows it.'

'Yeah,' said Lucy. 'I think he knows he blew it with you before.'

'Yeah,' said Nesta, 'you have to tell him how you feel now. And Ollie, too. I think through all of this you've been putting them first. How they feel. What they want. Your feelings matter too, TJ. What you want.'

Nesta is so top, I thought. It was so kind of her to say what she just did and not hold any grudges about what happened in the beginning with Luke and I.

'So what are you going to say to Luke?' asked Izzie.

'Oh, I don't know. It wasn't just my fault that things went wrong . . . I don't know. I'll see how it comes out. I will try and tell him how I feel. Oh God*dddd*. Do I have to do it now?'

The thought of talking to Luke filled me with dread. What if what I wanted to say came out all wrong? What if we misunderstood each other again? I couldn't bear it.

Nesta stood up. 'Izzie, Lucy – in the kitchen. TJ,' she said, and then pointed to the phone on her bedside cabinet. 'Phone, and you're not allowed out until you've done them all. Luke. Cat. Ollie.'

'God, you're bossy!' I said.

Nesta grinned. 'Thanks.'

Lucy got off my back. 'She's right, though. Get it over with.'

Izzie got up and gave me the thumbs up.

And off they went.

I stared at the phone for a few moments, then got my notepad out of my bag. Who to call first?

I checked the numbers, then dialled.

Mrs Biasi's voice on their answering machine told me that no one was home. I tried Luke's mobile. It was on voicemail.

I dialled the next number.

'Hello,' said a young boy's voice a moment later.

'Er, is Cat there please?'

'CAAATTTTTTTTTTTT,' the boy yelled at the other end. He was so loud he almost shattered my eardrum.

I heard footsteps. 'Hello?'

I took a deep breath and launched in.

'Hi Cat, it's me, TJ, the girl you met on the beach and I'm sorry that I didn't tell you at the time but I am the girl that Ollie was seeing behind your back but please can we be friends? I didn't know that he had a girlfriend down there and if I had known I wouldn't have gone out with him because I don't like boys who are two-timers. I don't two-time people . . . and I don't want you to think that I'm a boyfriend stealer because I'm not. I genuinely didn't know about you.'

There was a silence at the other end.

'Cat. Are you there? Say something.'

'Oh, sorry,' said Cat. 'My stupid brother was at the door trying to listen in so I had to shoo him away. Yeah, you were saying about Ollie. Yeah. I thought there was someone else, so it's good to know that I'm not crazy and imagining things. And yeah, I knew what he was like. He never said that we were an item as in girlfriend and boyfriend. It was always understood that we'd hang out in a casual way. So . . . are you going to see him again?'

'Don't think so. Not on his terms. I'll be totally honest. I was starting to like him a lot but I don't think I could continue if I knew that he was seeing other girls as well. It would do my head in.'

Cat laughed. 'Tell me about it. Have you told him you met me?'

'Not yet. I haven't spoken to him since I got back. But I will tell him. You bet I will.'

Cat laughed again. 'Hah. I'd love to be a fly on the wall when you speak to him! Listen, TJ, I'm cool. You do what you have to. I have no expectations of Ollie Axford, and to be totally honest with you back, I was thinking of calling it a day with him anyway. Same reason as you. He does my head in. It was fun for a while, but we weren't really going anywhere. I think he's one of those boys who likes a challenge, you know? He's not ready to have a proper relationship, and I am. I want more and I know that I'll never get it from him.'

'That's exactly how I feel. We deserve more than to be a number amongst many in his little black book.'

'Yeah. Right on, TJ. Us girls rule, yeah?'

'Yeah. But Cat, listen, my mates are really into coming down in the summer so I hope that we can meet up again. I hope that we can all be friends.'

'Yeah, sure,' said Cat. 'I'd like that. And now that you've called I *know* that we could be friends. That you're an honest person. To be doubly, trebly honest, after I'd met you, I saw my mates down here, you know, Becca and Ollie's sister, Lia. I said I'd met this great girl on the beach called TJ and Lia went pale. I asked why and if she knew you or something and, well, Lia can't lie to save her life and she told me that she thought Ollie had been seeing someone called TJ. So I did know it was you in the end. But I'm really glad you called and told me yourself.'

'I should have done it on the beach but . . . sometimes I panic and I was scared you'd hate me.'

'Nah,' said Cat. 'I wouldn't have hated you, although I have to admit I was a bit jealous when I found out. OK, a lot jealous, but then again it showed me what being involved with Ollie would always be like. I don't want to get in too deep with him if it's forever going to throw up that kind of emotion. I want to move on from that and find some guy who adores me and only me and doesn't need to see other people. Know what I mean?'

'Exactly,' I said. 'I can't do the casual thing either. You know, it's funny. Ollie told me all about Lia and I really wanted to meet her, but she was never there when we went up to the house. Now I know why. I guess he didn't want us to meet because he knew she was a mate of yours.'

'Probably. So listen, I've got to go . . . My dad's doing supper and it smells like he's burned something as usual. Stay in touch and see you in the summer, hey?'

'Will do,' I said. 'And good luck finding the right guy.'

'You too, TJ.'

We swapped e-mail addresses and promised to stay in touch. I felt so much better when I put down the phone. I'd been dreading the call, but Cat was cool about the whole situation. And talking to her had made it much clearer what I felt about Ollie. I did like him, but she was right – a relationship with him could never go anywhere. He was a player, and involvement with him would always be a rollercoaster of emotions. Not for me, I thought, as I dialled Luke's mobile again.

It was still on voicemail. I didn't leave a message.

I was about to dial Ollie's number, but then I thought, no, I'd text him. Cool. Calm. Collected.

HI OLY. BK IN LNDN. MET CAT IN CRNWL. CU L8R.

I was about to send it when I thought, no, I'm being a coward again. I can do this. My feelings matter too, and I need to express them. I need to come clean with him and talk to him in person.

I deleted my message and dialled his mobile.

'Hello, stranger,' he said.

'Er, hi, yeah. It's TJ.'

Ollie laughed. 'I know that. I know your voice. Plus your number came up on my mobile. So when did you get back?'

'Earlier. Listen, Ollie, I need to ask you something.'

'Shoot.'

'Er . . . do you have a girlfriend down in Cornwall?'

He was silent for a moment. 'Why do you ask?'

'Oh just . . . well, we never talked about stuff like that. For all I know you may be engaged or have been with someone for ages.'

Ollie laughed again. 'Actually, I'm married with four kids, but I didn't want to tell you in case it put you off.'

'Seriously, Ollie. I need to know.'

'Right. OK. Serious. Do I have a girlfriend in Cornwall? Yes. I have a few girls who are friends in Cornwall. And a few more up here.'

'You know what I mean. *Girlfriend* girlfriend.'

'You mean as in exclusive?'

'Yes.'

'No.'

'OK, so who's Cat then?'

'Ah. Now I'm beginning to get the picture . . .'

'So am I. We met on the beach in Cawsand and . . . well, put it this way, put two and two together.'

'Cat's a mate,' said Ollie. 'A good mate. We never said we wouldn't see anyone else.'

'I know. She told me that.'

'So what's the problem?'

'Well, what about us?' I asked. 'Are we just mates?'

I could hear Ollie sigh at the other end of the phone. Tough, I thought. I know boys hate conversations like this, but I didn't care. I wanted to know what he had to say.

'What about us? I don't know, TJ. We're having a good time, aren't we? Hanging out.'

'Yes.'

'And I told you that I really liked you. I meant it. I think you're really cool. What else do you want?'

I had to think for a moment. What did I want from Ollie? Commitment? To be his one and only? And he to be mine? I wasn't sure. All I knew was that I didn't want to be one of many.

'Actually, I don't want anything,' I said. 'At least, not anything you can give at the present time, I don't think. It's cool. It really is. I just wanted to know where we stood. Where I stood. So thanks. Thanks for being honest.'

'Anytime. So now you're back, want to get together next week?'

'Er . . . probably not,' I said. 'I'll be honest, too. I can't do the let's hang out and see where it goes type of thing. You were beginning to be more than a mate to me, and if you don't feel the same way then I can't see the point of us hanging out. It would do my head in. So sorry, no can do.'

'Oh,' said Ollie. He sounded surprised. 'But . . .'

'Later,' I said. 'I really enjoyed the time we spent together.'

'Me too. But . . .' Ollie stuttered.

'Later, hey.'

And then I hung up. It felt great to have said what I wanted to and not to worry about what he did or didn't think. Nesta was right. My feelings mattered too, and my main feeling was that I wanted a guy who wanted me and me alone.

Phew, I thought as I put the phone back. Done. Dusted.

Almost.

I got up to go and find the others in the kitchen, but when I got there, it was empty. The French doors leading to Nesta's garden were open and I could hear voices.

I followed the sound of the voices and found Izzie, Lucy, Nesta and William standing by the gate that led to the road. They all looked very shifty.

'Ah, TJ. Er . . . finished?' asked Nesta.

'Almost,' I said. 'Hi, William.'

William shuffled about on his feet as if he was uncomfortable about something. 'Er . . . hi,' he said. 'Er . . .'

'Yes. Right,' said Nesta. 'We're just going down the shop to get some . . . milk.'

'Yes. Milk,' said Izzie and opened the gate.

What was going on? I wondered. Everyone was acting very strangely.

'I'll come with you,' said Lucy as she went to join Izzie. 'Later, TJ.'

'But I'll come too,' I said.

'No!' said Nesta. 'You stay here. In case . . . er, we're expecting a delivery. Can you stay and open the door?'

'But where's your mum and dad? And Tony?'

'All out,' said Nesta as she hauled William out of the back gate. 'Go, TJ. Back inside. Go. Inside. Go. Answer door.'

'But . . . hey, can't one of you stay with me?' I called after them.

Izzie shrugged. 'We've got to get a *lot* of milk,' she said, then sniggered and disappeared behind the hedge besides the gate.

And then I heard them all laughing.

What on earth were they up to?

After they'd gone, I went back into the flat and went to sit in the living room. I was flicking through a magazine when I heard the front doorbell go.

Ah, the mysterious delivery, I thought, as I got up to answer.

I went into the hall and opened the door.

It wasn't a delivery.

It was Luke.

Don't put off until tomorrow what you can do today.

# Chapter 15

# Summer
# Sizzler

'I think Dad might have had a personality transplant the last time he was in the hospital,' I said as I watched Dad in the garden. He was wearing a Homer Simpson apron and was busy cooking sausages (vegetarian soya!) and chicken legs on the barbecue. 'Either that or he's been taken over by aliens.'

'Well, he looks the same,' said Izzie, 'but you're right, there is something different, and I don't just mean the apron.'

'He's smiling,' said Lucy. 'That's what it is.'

'Yeah,' said Nesta. 'And at us, too. It's worrying, isn't it?'

We'd been back in London a week, and Dad had been acting peculiarly from the moment we got home.

On Monday while I was at school, he'd gone out with Mum and bought a barbecue and two mobile phones.

'His and hers,' he said with a grin as he held the phones up to show me. 'Latest technology. Man in the shop says it does everything. I can text on it, speak into it. I think it even turns into a helicopter if I can only work out how to use it.'

'And the barbecue?' I asked. 'You always disapproved of them. Excuse to undercook meat and make a lot of noise that annoys the neighbours you always said.'

'I'm a new man,' said Dad. 'Life is short. Seize the day and all that, that's my new philosophy. So this Saturday, invite all your friends. Lucy and Nesta and Izzie. And their parents. And be sure to ask that nice Mr Lovering who owns the health shop. See if he can come with his wife. Yes. We'll have a party.'

It was then that I knew something was seriously wrong. Dad didn't do barbecues. He didn't do parties. If by any chance he had to attend a social gathering, he'd put himself in a corner from where he would scowl and be grumpy and growl at people.

But buying the barbecue and phones was only the start of his new persona.

On Tuesday, after talking to his solicitor, he put in an offer on Rose Harbour cottage. 'Looks like it's in the bag,' he said when I got home from school. 'We have us a holiday home. I'll put on the kettle and we can celebrate. Oh ha ha, I'll put on the kettle, bet it won't suit me.'

Mum and I exchanged anxious looks. Dad making jokes? Even making bad ones was a novelty for him.

On Wednesday, I returned home wondering what he'd have bought that day while I was out. I wasn't disappointed. He'd got us cable TV.

'Seventy channels plus all the film channels,' he said.

'But Dad, you always said that people have better things to do with their time than sit about watching TV,' I said.

'Changed my mind,' he said, grinning. 'Now that I'm going to be relaxing a bit more, I can catch up with all the movies I've missed over the years. And I'm going to get myself one of those comfy footstools so that I can put my feet up while I'm doing it.'

Thursday and Friday were even stranger. I found him with his nose in recipe books preparing for Saturday. Dad had never so much as boiled an egg before and now, today, he was out there being King of the Barbecue, with a big smile on his face, handing out drinks, cooking fish and meat and discussing how to marinate a courgette with Lucy's dad.

Miracles will never cease.

Everybody came. Lucy's mum and dad. Her brothers, Steve and Lal. Nesta's mum and dad. Tony. Izzie's mum and her stepfather Angus. And William. And Luke.

When I'd found him standing on the doorstep at Nesta's last week, I soon realised that I'd been set up. To begin with it had felt awkward and neither of us seemed to know what to say. It was Luke who'd plunged in first.

'I'm so sorry about the other week,' he said. 'You must have thought I was a total jerk.'

'Not really,' I said. 'I . . . well . . . OK, I did. You didn't let me explain. See, Ollie . . . I only met him a short time ago. We weren't even seriously dating or anything. I . . .'

'I know. I jumped to all the wrong conclusions. I'm so sorry. I thought you'd set me up . . .'

'What, like Nesta did to both of us just now?'

Luke smiled. 'Yeah. Er . . . hope you don't mind. I asked her to let me know when you were back. I've been thinking about you all week and . . .'

He was looking at me with such tenderness, I felt myself starting to melt.

'I wouldn't have set you up to hurt you,' I said. 'I'm not like that.'

'I know. I should have known. I . . .'

I took a step towards him. I couldn't help it. Whenever he was in close proximity he was like a magnet, and I was helpless to resist. 'One question, Luke,' I said as we stood so close I could see how black and dilated his pupils were.

'Sure. Anything.'

'Is there anyone else in your life at the moment. I mean, any other girls?'

'No. Same question to you. Is there in your life?'

I was about to say, no, no girls in my life either, but it didn't feel like the time for jokes. It felt too intense. Serious. I shook my head.

Luke sighed with relief and smiled. 'Good,' he said, 'because I think we got off to a bad start. Me being with Nesta and even before that a whole load of different girls. But I knew there was something special as soon as I met you. I'd really like to spend more time with you, TJ. Get to know you better. That is, if you'd like to.'

I couldn't bear it any longer. I put my arms around his neck and kissed him.

A few seconds later, I heard the sound of cheering. Izzie, Lucy, Nesta and William were all standing at the front gate grinning like idiots. I don't believe it, I thought. Will we *ever* get a chance to snog without being interrupted?

We did.

Monday after school.

Tuesday after school.

Wednesday after Luke's shift at the restaurant.

Thursday before Luke went off to his acting class.

Friday before we both went off to catch up on homework.

And today he came to the barbecue and met Mum and Dad and just about everyone else I know. This time we're out in the open. A couple. No secrets.

As we sat around the garden, our plates piled high with burgers and salads and baked potatoes, I looked around me. The sun was shining down. The forecast was that it was going to continue and we were in for a sizzling summer. Lucy with Tony, Nesta with William. Luke chatting away to Izzie. Everyone seemed to be smiling. This is one of those precious moments, I thought. I'm with the people I love. Everyone is well. Who knows what the future holds for any of us? All we can be sure of is that everything changes. Life never stays still. Up and down we go. People come and go into our lives. Boys come and go into our lives.

I noticed Lucy looking at me quizzically.

'What are you thinking, TJ?' she asked.

'Oh you know, just that everything changes . . .'

'Some things,' she said, and put her hand on the table. 'But some things stay the same. Like us guys. Mates forever.'

I put my hand over hers. 'Mates forever,' I said.

Izzie put her hand over mine.

And Nesta put hers over Izzie's.

I looked up at the sky. I don't know much about what's out there or where it all came from or why. And I still don't know if there's anyone like a God up there after space or in some heaven looking down. But I do know that here, where I am, planet earth, this three-dimensional wonderland, life can be good sometimes. So my philosophy is going to be Hannah's philosophy. Dad's new philosophy. To seize the day. Appreciate. Enjoy life. To experience it all to the best of my ability, and maybe the big questions will get answered along the way. Maybe. Maybe not. In the meantime, there's the rest of the summer to look forward to. A holiday in Cornwall. I've got a great family and the best bunch of mates ever. I must always remember to let them know that's what I think while we are all here. And not just on days like this.

I looked down at the table.

Four hands. Four friends. Forever.

E-mail: **Inbox (1)**
To: <u>babewithbrains@psnet.co.uk</u>
From: <u>grooviechick@firstmail.com</u>
Date: 10th June
Subject: Summer

Hey TJ,
Spoke to Mac. Told him all about you. There are rooms free at his mum's place in July and August, so we're all set for your visit down here. The long-range weather is for hot and hotter. Hope you're still planning to come. My mates can't wait to meet yours, and Mac is already having fantasies about Izzie. Tee hee.

Cat
XXX

It may be the end of the Mates, Dates series, but Lucy, Nesta, Izzie and TJ are starting to appear in Cathy Hopkins's other series TRUTH, DARE, KISS OR PROMISE!

LOVE LOTTERY sees the Mates, Dates characters take a trip to the Rame Peninsula where one of them gets a most unusual welcome! The London crowd soon discover that they have a lot in common with the Cornish gang and Becca in particular finds that her new friends can help her through a turbulent time in her life.

And in the very last TRUTH, DARE, KISS OR PROMISE book – ALL MATES TOGETHER – Lucy, Nesta, Izzie and TJ spend a few weeks in the summer with Cat and her friends Lia, Mac, Squidge and Becca. Romance is definitely on the cards!

# Also available by Cathy Hopkins

## The Mates, Dates series

1. Mates, Dates and Inflatable Bras
2. Mates, Dates and Cosmic Kisses
3. Mates, Dates and Portobello Princesses
4. Mates, Dates and Sleepover Secrets
5. Mates, Dates and Sole Survivors
6. Mates, Dates and Mad Mistakes
7. Mates, Dates and Pulling Power
8. Mates, Dates and Tempting Trouble
9. Mates, Dates and Great Escapes
10. Mates, Dates and Chocolate Cheats
11. Mates, Dates and Diamond Destiny
12. Mates, Dates and Sizzling Summers

*Companion Books:*
Mates, Dates Guide to Life
Mates, Dates and You
Mates, Dates Journal

## The Truth, Dare, Kiss or Promise series

1. White Lies and Barefaced Truths
2. Pop Princess
3. Teen Queens and Has-Beens
4. Starstruck
5. Double Dare
6. Midsummer Meltdown
7. Love Lottery
8. All Mates Together

## The Cinnamon Girl series

1. This Way to Paradise
2. Starting Over

**Find out more at www.piccadillypress.co.uk**
**Join Cathy's Club at www.cathyhopkins.com**

# www.piccadillypress.co.uk

☆ The latest news on forthcoming books

☆ Chapter previews

☆ Author biographies

☆ Fun quizzes

☆ Reader reviews

☆ Competitions and fab prizes

☆ Book features and cool downloads

☆ And much, much more . . .

## Log on and check it out!

*Piccadilly Press*